Nov. 28⁺ᵉ
1984.

Book of Shotguns

James Marchington

BOOK OF SHOTGUNS

PELHAM BOOKS

To Sara

First published in Great Britain by
Pelham Books Ltd
44 Bedford Square
London WC1B 3DU
1984

©1984 by James Marchington

British Library Cataloguing in Publication Data
Marchington, James
  Book of shotguns.
  1. Shotguns—History
  I. Title
  683.4′26′09   TS536.8

ISBN 0-7207-1516-4

Photoset, printed and bound by
Butler & Tanner Limited, Frome, Somerset

Contents

ACKNOWLEDGEMENTS

The author and publishers are grateful to the following for permission to reproduce copyright photographs: Hull Cartridge Co. pages 32, 36; James Marchington pages 21, 30, 60, 67, 79, 81, 84, 87, 91, 94, 96, 103, 104, 109; John Marchington pages 40, 41, 46, 50, 52, 74, 76, 80, 83, 88, 93, 98, 99; David Nickerson (Tathwell) Ltd. pages 10, 22, 25, 86; Parker-Hale pages 18, 42, 103; Sara Pinhorn pages viii, 16, 87(top); W. & C. Scott pages 5, 6, 9, 13, 44, 66; *Shooting Magazine* pages 56, 107, 108; Smith & Wesson page 28; Winchester U.K. pages 33, 78.

The proof marks on pages 112 and 113 are reproduced from copy supplied by Eley Ltd. and the British marks are by courtesy of the Worshipful Company of Gunmakers and the Birmingham Gun Barrel Proof House.

PART I

GUNS

1. The side-by-side has the advantage of being easy to carry when walking long distances in search of your quarry.

1 The side-by-side

The side-by-side is far and away the most popular type of shotgun used for rough and game shooting in Britain today – and has been so for a couple of hundred years. At any of the game shoots in this country during the season, the chances are that you will see nothing but side-by-sides. These guns are built to the traditional English pattern, which has evolved over the years to suit British field shooting conditions. It is far less likely that all the guns you will see were actually made in Britain, however, because foreign gunmakers – particularly in Spain – now produce acceptable alternatives at very competitive prices.

The reason for the side-by-side's popularity is a curious mixture of common sense and prejudice. It is true that the design is well suited to the demands of British game shooters, but some others are not far wide of the mark. Perhaps the strongest reason of all is that game shooters feel that 'this is the type of gun that my grandfather used, and it's good enough for me'. I shall discuss the arguments for and against these guns later in this chapter, but for the moment let us look at the very finest examples of the type – the 'best' English guns produced by the old established names of gunmaking: names such as Purdey, Holland & Holland, Boss and many more.

These guns represent the peak of the gunmaker's art, and many people would argue that they are truly perfect. It would certainly be virtually impossible to improve on them. Built by craftsmen from the finest materials available, they are a delight to use and beautiful to look at. They are made with no constraints on cost; the customer demands the finest quality that can be achieved, and he is prepared to pay whatever is necessary to achieve it.

This perfection in design as well as materials and workmanship was not arrived at by chance, of course. Each tiny part of a 'best' English gun, from the bead foresight to the carefully fitted stock, has evolved over the years to perform its job as well as possible. All excess weight has been removed, for example, leaving the gun light enough to handle well yet with enough weight to keep recoil down to an acceptable level.

The design of the side-by-side was really perfected around one hundred years ago, and there have been few alterations since. The few remaining top English gunmakers are still making guns virtually identical to those built at the end of the nineteenth century. What has changed during that time is the conditions under which the guns are used – but that is another story.

Many of the finest guns made in Britain today are bought by customers in the Middle East and the United States, and these countries have played a considerable part in keeping our gunmaking trade on its feet. However, other examples of this type of gun find their way into the hands of our Royal Family, wealthy farmers or businessmen so it would be wrong to assume that all the guns made by our top gunmakers go to wealthy foreigners.

When a gun is built by hand from top quality materials, it is bound to be more expensive than the average shooter can afford. The current basic price of a 'best' London gun is somewhere in the region of ten thousand pounds (in 1984), and this figure can easily be doubled or even trebled if the customer wants more elaborate decoration such as engraving, gold inlay and so on. Most shooters can only dream of owning such a gun; but people do exist who are prepared to pay the price for the finest gun that money can buy. The order books at Purdey's in London, for example, are generally full for two and a half years in advance, and they produce around seventy guns a year.

Many of these guns will never see a muddy field or the back of a Land-Rover. Their investment value is such that they are often kept securely in a bank vault, while their owners shoot with one of the many cheaper alternatives. To me this seems a terrible shame. A best gun is not a valuable trinket – it is a superbly functional piece of machinery, with a life of its own breathed into it by the craftsmen who made it. To appreciate it fully, you must use it for its original purpose.

All 'best' guns are built specifically to suit the individual customer, with all the measurements calculated so that the gun fits precisely in his shoulder and comes on aim as naturally as pointing a finger. The first step in buying a 'best' gun, therefore, is to discuss your requirements with your gunmaker. There are many details to be decided on, such as the barrel length, chambers and chokes, type of trigger and style of engraving. The gunmaker will also measure the customer to ensure a perfect fit. He will normally use a try gun, which can be adjusted to give various degrees of bend and cast-off as well as different stock lengths. The subject of gun fitting is explored in more detail in chapter 7.

Different companies of gunmakers differ in their exact methods, which are handed down from one generation to the next, but most follow the same basic principles. In the larger companies, individual craftsmen specialise in a particular part of the finished gun, serving an apprenticeship of five years or more before qualifying. In the smaller firms, producing no more than a pair or two a year, one man may see the gun right through from start to finish.

The work can be divided into four main steps: barrelling, actioning, stocking and finishing.

Barrelling

The barreller starts with solid steel rods, selected for the quality and type of metal. These are cut to the correct length before being bored out to an internal diameter which is slightly smaller than the eventual bore of the gun. The outside of the tubes is then 'struck down' or turned to the required diameter. The rods will have a 'lump' at the breech end, and these lumps are machined to approximately their final dimensions at this stage. It is essential that the barreller bores the tubes straight and true, so that the barrel walls are of even thickness. Off-centre bores will weaken the walls, which could result in the barrel bursting when it is tested in the Proof House.

The next step is to 'lap' the bores, which means increasing their internal diameter to the required dimensions. The muzzle end is left with a slight constriction, depending on the degree of choke required. The chambers are then made, and the barrels polished inside and out. The pair of barrels must also be joined together, carefully aligned so that they will shoot to the same point of aim. The ribs are fitted, and the fore-end loop brazed on. It is common practice at this stage for the gunmaker to submit the barrels to the London or Birmingham Proof House for Provisional Proof. At the Proof House, the barrels are fired with abnormally heavy loads of powder and shot to test their strength. Any flaws in materials or manufacture will show up under the stress of Proofing, and the gunmaker will not waste time and money by continuing work on faulty barrels.

Actioning

The next stage is to make and fit the action. A 'best' English gun will invariably be a sidelock, in which the mechanism for firing each barrel is fitted to a separate plate – one on either side of the gun. The action also incorporates the device for cocking the mechanism, the safety catch, and a means of locking the barrels in the closed position for firing.

The firing mechanism comprises the tumbler or hammer, which is held in the cocked position against the pressure of the mainspring by a sear. The sear is disengaged by pulling the trigger blade, allowing the tumbler to fall and strike the firing pin. This delivers a sharp blow to the cap of the cartridge, causing it to ignite. Each part of the action is carefully shaped and fitted, so that the mechanism works smoothly and reliably. Every part must be correctly hardened, too, to give the necessary combination of strength and elasticity. The design of the action, like the rest of the gun, has been improved over the years to eliminate points of potential weakness.

The action is fitted to the barrels, using the traditional method of blacking the metal surfaces with a candle or paraffin flame to show up the 'high spots' where metal rubs against metal. By carefully striking off the excess metal with a file, the craftsman can achieve amazing tolerances – within the diameter of a soot particle.

Once the action is fitted to the barrels, the gun is normally returned to the Proof House for Final Proof before going on to the stocker. Appendix I gives details of the Proof Marks that are used and accepted in this country. Proof is a valuable test of a gun's ability to withstand normal use, and it is compulsory under British law. The Proof Marks of certain other countries are accepted here under a reciprocal agreement, but there are important exceptions. An offence is committed if you sell or attempt to sell a gun that is 'out of Proof'. This is an additional reason, apart from sheer safety, for making sure that you understand the rules and marks before buying or selling any shotgun.

Stocking

At this stage, the gun is described as being 'in the white', because the metal is still in its shiny, unfinished state. The stocker begins work on a selected walnut blank that has been seasoned for many months. The wood is chosen for its grain, which must run straight through the hand of the stock to confer sufficient strength, and should form an attractive pattern in the rearward part. The fore-end is chosen to match the stock, of course. All this means that only a small part of each tree is suitable for gun stocking, which naturally adds to the cost. Finding pieces that match for a pair of guns is even more difficult.

2. A craftsman working on the chambers of a pair of barrels from a side-by-side shotgun.

3. Mr P.G. Whatley, Managing Director of W. & C. Scott, examines an action 'in the white'.

The wood is seasoned to allow the excess moisture to evaporate, so that the stock will not warp, shrink or change weight after the gun is finished. Blanks are stored in carefully controlled conditions, and each one is weighed at regular intervals and the weight recorded. The stocker will not begin work on a blank until the weight has remained stable for several months.

The stock is fitted perfectly to the metal of the action, so that moisture is kept out and the recoil is distributed over the widest possible area, so reducing the chance of the wood splitting. The stocker must also take care that the wood does not catch the working parts of the action, and prevent them operating correctly. The stock is then bent to the exact measurements specified on the customer's order. It is heated, normally with infra-red lamps, until it can be moulded to give precisely the right amount of cast-off and bend, and then left to set in this position.

Finishing

When the stock is ready, the engraver begins work on the action. Depending on the order, this may be a simple scroll design or a more complicated pattern, sometimes including game scenes or even the customer's favourite dog. Special guns may be made to commemorate anniversaries or events, and these give the engraver enormous scope to exercise his talents. The most ornate guns will have gold inlay to highlight the main features of the design. Even the simplest floral scroll engraving on a 'best' gun could take a skilled engraver a fortnight to complete, while more complicated work might keep him fully occupied for several months.

When the engraver has finished, the action is polished and then case hardened to strengthen the metal and produce the attractive mother-of-pearl colouring that is characteristic of a well made gun. It is not easy to achieve good-looking, bright colours, since this requires skilful application of heat and oil if the finish is not to appear dull and uninteresting. The metal parts that are not case hardened – the trigger guard, safety catch and top lever – are normally blacked to give a rust-resistant finish that contrasts well with the polished action.

The gun is then test fired at a pattern plate – a sheet of metal painted with whitewash – to check the patterns. Patterning is an art in itself, and it must be done under strictly controlled conditions in order to produce valid results. The distance from the muzzles to the plate must be measured accurately, for instance, and the bores must be dirtied by firing a couple of shots before the tests are made. Clean or oily bores would give misleading patterns.

The gunmaker regulates the patterns by altering the degree of choke and the angle of the choke cone. Some control over the patterns is also possible by working on the chamber cone. Choke is defined by the percentage of the pellets contained within a 30-inch (76 centimetres) circle at a range of 40 yards (36.5 metres); but there is a lot more to regulating chokes than simply achieving the required pattern percentage. The pellets must be spread evenly across the pattern, with the minimum of dense spots and open patches through which a bird could escape unharmed. The gun will normally be regulated with the brand of cartridge and shot size specified by the customer, because the results will vary with different loads. This subject is examined in detail in chapter 8.

At this stage, the customer will normally be invited to examine the work so far, and the gun's fit will be checked. This is necessary in case he has lost or gained weight, or requires the original specifications to be changed for some other reason. If all is well, the stock will be chequered, and any final balancing done by boring holes into the butt of the stock and inserting lead weights. The wood is then polished with a traditional mixture of linseed and other oils, applied in a number of coats each of which is laboriously rubbed in by hand. The barrels receive a final polishing, and are then blacked in a bath of salts to give a rich, deep lustre. The gun is checked, and any minor imperfections corrected. Finally, it is fitted into its case ready for the customer – some three years or more since he first set foot in the gunmaker's shop.

The amount of time spent by highly skilled craftsmen in making a 'best' English gun ensures that its price is high. Such guns are works of art as well as supremely functional weapons, however, and to those with an eye for quality they are worth every penny. For most of us, it is more practical to consider one of the cheaper alternatives from this country or abroad. It is worth noting that 'best' English guns are highly regarded all over the world, and they fetch high prices from investors and collectors in specialist auctions – particularly in the London salerooms of firms such as Christie's.

It is a sad fact that little remains today of the gunmaking trade that once flourished in Britain. Fewer than five hundred shotguns are made each year in this country, compared to the eighty thousand or so per annum in the early part of this century. Of those firms that remain, W. & C. Scott of Birmingham produce the largest number of guns – making more than two hundred double-barrelled shotguns each year and about seven hundred of their single-barrelled Greener GP model which is described in chapter 5.

Whereas the 'best' English guns are sidelocks, W. & C. Scott concentrate on boxlocks. This type of gun has the working parts contained in a box-shaped action instead of on separate lock plates. This means that the works can be a little more tricky to get at if something should go wrong, although some people would argue that a boxlock is inherently more simple and therefore more reliable than a sidelock. In practice, the differences can be ignored. Both types of side-by-side will last several lifetimes provided they are properly made and carefully looked after.

The boxlock is generally cheaper to produce, and tends to be associated with the relatively less expensive weapons. It is still possible to spend several thousand pounds on a boxlock. One of the most obvious differences between boxlock and sidelock is in the outward appearance. I personally feel that the sidelock looks better, with its flowing lines evolved from the old hammer guns. Boxlocks can be made to look very attractive, however, and some are even fitted with dummy sideplates just to confuse the issue.

A small number of other firms in Britain, both in Birmingham and in other parts of the country, still produce side-by-side shotguns. Many of the smaller firms today do not in fact produce the guns from the raw materials, but buy them 'in the white' from the larger manufacturers – and simply finish them to the customer's specifications on their own premises. This is not a modern development in the trade, however. Today's collectors are frequently confused by guns bearing the name of a small provincial gunsmith, when they were actually made by the London or Birmingham factory of a more widely known company.

The vast majority of side-by-side shotguns used today in Britain and

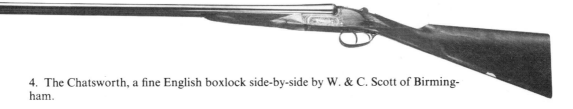

4. The Chatsworth, a fine English boxlock side-by-side by W. & C. Scott of Birmingham.

elsewhere come not from Britain, the traditional home of these guns, but from the Continent – particularly Spain. For various reasons, gunmakers in that country can produce guns to relatively high standards at very competitive prices. The result is value for money that Britain's manufacturers cannot match. The Spanish gunmakers' success is due largely to their use of advanced, modern mechanised production methods. Economies of scale play a part, too. They can strike a hard bargain when buying raw materials from their suppliers, and their overheads are spread more thinly since they are producing guns by the thousand rather than by the pair.

This is not to say that Spanish guns are necessarily inferior to their British made counterparts – certainly not in performance. I have used a Spanish AyA No.2 12 bore sidelock side-by-side for years, and it has served me well in all kinds of conditions. With it, I have shot virtually every British game species, and I also used it to shoot my first ever 25-straight at clay pigeons. With reasonable care and maintenance, I expect it to work well for many years to come, and it will almost certainly outlive me. The wood to metal fit is not perfect, and the tool marks show here and there, but it cost a fraction of the price of a 'best' English gun, and I don't suppose I would have killed a single extra bird if I had been using a Purdey.

5. The engraving on a Lincoln boxlock side-by-side.

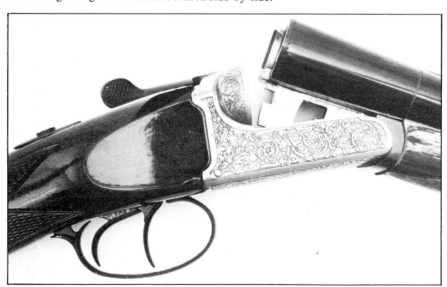

So why does anyone pay the price of a 'best' gun when alternatives such as this are available? There are many factors, of course, including the investment value, but most important is the satisfaction of owning and using one of the finest shotguns available. If I could afford to, I would buy one, knowing full well that I would be most unlikely to shoot even the tiniest bit better with it. But I would take great pleasure in its fine balance and handling, and I would admire the quality of its chequering and engraving as I waited for my quarry to appear.

The difference in price is way out of proportion to the difference in quality, however. Spanish and other large foreign gunmakers reduce their costs wherever possible by using machines to do those jobs that a man could do no better. They will machine a part to within a few thousandths of an inch of its eventual dimensions, making the final alterations by hand. In contrast, a traditional gunmaker might do the entire job by hand, without making the part any more accurately – at least in theory. Nevertheless, you would have a hard job to convince me that a top London gunmaker does not produce his guns more precisely – which must ultimately be reflected in their performance and reliability.

While on the subject of gun quality and price, I should mention the value of side-by-sides as an investment. In the past, good quality English side-by-sides have tended to increase in value at an astonishing rate, sometimes out-performing items that are thought of as good investments. This is treacherous ground for the uninitiated, however, and it is important to recognise that, while some weapons are likely to become more valuable as time goes by, others may prove to be an expensive mistake.

The problem is how to tell one from the other, and it is impossible to cover such a complicated subject comprehensively within the confines of this book. I do not pretend to be an expert on gun values, but the basic principles are well understood. Any gun is worth no more than what someone is prepared to pay for it, and the guns that are most consistently in demand are quality side-by-sides from known English makers. That said, it would be wrong to assume that any gun bearing the name of Boss, Atkin or Holland, for example, is worth a fortune. The vital factors are quality and condition. A good quality gun that has suffered neglect and misuse will be worth little, despite the 'big name' engraved on its sideplates. Conversely, a good, solid, run-of-the-mill weapon by a less well known maker could be valuable

11

in good condition. The gun's age is practically irrelevant, which may seem strange in these nostalgic times when almost anything that merits the description 'antique' seems to fetch a pretty penny. With shotguns, however, it is only when you go back to the days of muzzle loaders that the gun's age becomes a significant factor. There are a few exceptions, of course, such as when a particular weapon has some special merit or interest – produced to mark a Royal anniversary, for instance.

As I write, in the summer of 1983, worldwide recession has hit the gun trade as hard as any other, and British dealers in particular are finding the market somewhat depressed – although there are a few hopeful signs that things may pick up. The result is that the lower classes of gun are not selling well, although sufficient buyers remain in the market to keep prices high for the very best examples of British craftsmanship.

Before buying a side-by-side, or any other type of gun for that matter, you should consider how much you are likely to use it, and to what extent you see it as an investment. There are plenty of other factors to consider, of course, but here I am referring only to the financial aspects. It would be foolish from this point of view to buy a brand new 'best' gun for extensive wildfowling and rough shooting, and to expect it to maintain its value. This is taking things to extremes, perhaps, but it serves to illustrate the point. Conversely, a sportsman who will take his gun to a few driven shoots a year, and will look after it carefully, would be well advised to buy the best he could afford.

I mentioned at the beginning of this chapter that side-by-sides are generally considered to be particularly suitable for game shooting, and it is worth looking at why this should be so. One of the most important factors is the weight and balance of a typical side-by-side gun. Most side-by-sides are relatively light in weight – between 6 and 7 pounds (3 and 4.5 kilogrammes). This means that they are easier to carry in the field, without being so light that they recoil uncomfortably with standard game cartridges loaded with 1 ounce (30 grammes) or $1\frac{1}{16}$ ounce (32 grammes) of shot. This question of weight naturally depends very largely on the type of shooting you do. A rough shooter who walks all day and fires perhaps no more than a dozen shots will probably be happy to use a light gun which would become uncomfortable if he fired many cartridges. He will put up with a fair amount of recoil for the benefit of carrying a lighter dead weight. On the other hand, a shooter decoying pigeons, or one who fired many shots at driven pheasants during the day's sport would be wise to choose a heavier weapon.

There are other advantages to using a side-by-side for game shooting. Its balance and quick handling suit the types of shot normally encountered in the field, and its clean lines are less likely to snag in undergrowth or clothing. The broad, flat bottom to the action is comfortable to carry in the crook of your arm, which is certainly not true of repeaters – and even an over-and-under can become uncomfortable if you carry it in this way for long.

The side-by-side is also easy to dismantle for cleaning and transporting by car. This is equally true of over-and-unders, of course, but there are other points where the side-by-side scores over the over-and-under for game shooting. Its design means that it opens to a relatively shallow angle when you extract or eject fired cartridge cases, for instance. This makes it faster to re-load, which can be important when game is coming over thick and fast – as in a grouse butt or on a busy stand at a pheasant drive. It is not always appreciated that a side-by-side fitted with ejectors has a greater capacity for sustained firepower than any other type of shotgun, including the semi-automatic. This rather makes a nonsense of the argument that sportsmen

6. The Chatsworth, one of W. & C. Scott's range of boxlocks named after historic country houses.

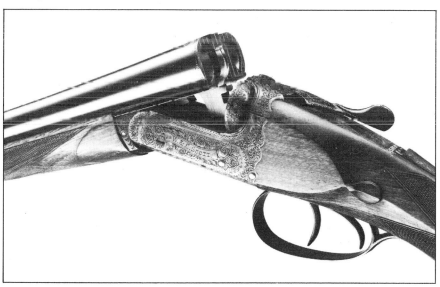

with repeaters are likely to slaughter large numbers of game. What matters is the attitude of the man behind the gun. Given a pair of ejector side-by-sides and an experienced loader, a shooter can maintain a phenomenal rate of fire.

So far I have made little mention of one of the most important reasons for choosing a side-by-side for game shooting. Quite simply, game shooters are a pretty conservative bunch, and they tend to regard any other type of gun as rather out of place on the game shoot. The over-and-under user is likely to encounter a few raised eyebrows, while a repeater of any sort is quite definitely beyond the pale. Not so long ago, I would have been inclined to challenge this attitude, presenting a well-reasoned argument against it. No amount of logic will overcome these deep-seated beliefs, however, and game shooting would not be the same without its quirks and traditions. Whatever your personal opinion on the subject, a conventional side-by-side is readily acceptable in any company. It is probably the wisest choice for the one gun man who plans to tackle various forms of shooting.

The prejudice of many sportsmen against other types of gun is based on sound enough principles, in fact. Apart from the advantages of the side-by-side that I have already mentioned, a break-barrel design is easy to make safe by opening the action when you cross an obstacle or stand chatting to your fellow guns. Most important, it is obvious to everyone around that your gun is safe, which is comforting to your companions – especially if they do not know you well. It is strange that many experienced shooters fail to take advantage of this, and leave their guns closed when in company. Their argument is that others should know that the gun is empty, and they can become quite offended at the suggestion that they may not be trusted. Personally, I feel very uncomfortable with a closed gun pointing at my feet – and many times I have been horrified to discover that the gun was in fact loaded all the time. This is inexcusable, and the argument that the safety catch may be on carries no weight at all. This device frequently does no more than lock the trigger blades so that they cannot be pulled accidentally. It does not always protect against a worn or faulty sear, which could slip and cause an accidental discharge.

Another advantage of the conventional side-by-side is that it gives you an instant choice of choke, particularly if fitted with double triggers. Most over-and-unders have a trigger selector of some sort, but this is slow to operate compared with slipping your finger from one trigger to the other. Even with a variable choke device, a repeater cannot offer anything like this versatility.

The reliability of side-by-sides is almost legendary, and there are cases on record of these guns being dug up or retrieved from the bottom of a river in working order. Few people keep a record of the number of cartridges that they fire, but some side-by-sides have fired an estimated million rounds or more with little sign of wear. The best over-and-unders might well approach or even equal the reliability of a good side-by-side, but repeaters are more prone to malfunction due to dirt or unsuitable cartridges.

In addition to these advantages, the side-by-side is more widely known and better understood around the world than any other type. As the standard weapon of shooters in Britain and elsewhere for hundreds of years, the side-by-side is backed by a formidable wealth of experience and knowledge. Any gun fitter should be able to achieve a good fit with a side-by-side, while he might be struggling with an over and under, let alone a repeater. Also, most repairs can be carried out quickly and easily on a side-by-side.

So it is no accident that the side-by-side has reached the position that it holds today, as the most commonly used shotgun for game shooting in all its various forms. It has evolved and developed over many years to meet the demands of shooters who subject their guns to harsh treatment and extensive use. The most wealthy shooters have looked for a gun that not only works faultlessly, but also is a work of art in its own right — and they have paid what is necessary to acquire the best. The side-by-side has stood the test of time well, and held its own against competition from cheaper alternatives which at first sight may appear to offer some advantages. It is unrivalled in its own field; but, as we shall see, other types have taken over the lead position for other forms of shooting.

On a personal note, my own AyA No. 2 side-by-side has seen regular use since I was fourteen years old. It has done me proud in situations as far apart as walking up grouse in the Scottish Highlands and competing in clay pigeon events such as the British Open Sporting Championship. If I had to choose a single gun with which to shoot for the rest of my life, it would certainly be a conventional side-by-side. The only break from tradition that I might ask for would be a set of screw-in choke tubes, which can nowadays be fitted to double-bar-relled guns and make the side-by-side even more versatile.

7. The author with his Rizzini over-and-under shotgun, in this case being used for grouse shooting.

2 The over-and-under

The other major type of shotgun, at least in Britain, is the over-and-under, in which the barrels are arranged vertically one above the other. The over-and-under is otherwise similar to the side-by-side in most respects. It has all the advantages of two barrels, and it hinges at the breech to allow loading.

The arrangement of the barrels confers certain advantages and disadvantages, making the over-and-under better suited to different types of sport. In particular, it is a good choice for clay pigeon shooting. It is also versatile enough to cope well with most other forms of the sport, and many people use an over-and-under as an all-round gun with considerable success.

The principle of having the barrels of a double barrelled gun one above the other is not new. Examples have been found that are hundreds of years old, but it is only comparatively recently that over-and-unders have been widely accepted by shooters. One of the main reasons for the over-and-under's growth in popularity is the rise of clay pigeon shooting as a sport in its own right, rather than as a form of practice and preparation for game shooting.

Manufacture

The vast majority of over-and-unders come from one of two countries, Italy and Japan, although there are notable exceptions such as the Belgian-made Browning range. Most shooters tend to think of over-and-unders as mass-produced weapons, manufactured down to a price rather than up to a standard as opposed to the traditional methods used by the makers of side-by-sides. This may be true of some over-and-unders, but there are a good many manufacturers who uphold strong traditions and strive for the highest possible standards. Equally, as I mentioned in the previous chapter, a large number of side-by-sides are mass-produced.

Browning, for example, combine new techniques with traditional methods to make their high quality over-and-unders. Their craftsmen black the knuckle of the action with soot to ensure a perfect fit with the barrels, in the same way as a traditional English gunmaker. This goes hand in hand with the most advanced, modern machinery and production methods. The result is a quality gun at a reasonable price.

The use of modern technology in gunmaking is probably most pronounced among the makers of over-and-unders, in fact, and the numbers of guns they produce are quite astonishing. Beretta make no fewer than a hundred and eighty thousand shotguns a year in their factory in the Brescia region of northern Italy, for example, as well as a vast number of rifles and pistols. This level of production is only possible by using a high level of mechanisation but Beretta, like other over-and-under manufacturers, pay great attention to quality control. There are some parts of the operation that must still be done by hand in order to achieve the required quality – chequering the stocks for the better grades of gun, for instance – but much of the work can be carried out by high speed machinery.

The various processes are monitored by the most up-to-date equipment, which measures tolerances every bit as accurately as a trained eye, and at many times the speed. An experienced gunmaker of the old school might be able to work as accurately as a computer controlled machine, but he certainly could not match its level of production.

Most over-and-unders are made on the monobloc principle, which means that the barrels are let into a block of metal that comprises the breech, locking lugs and hinge. This is similar to the process of re-

8. A Parker-Hale 700 series over-and-under shotgun.

sleeving, used by gunsmiths for many years to repair guns with damaged or badly pitted barrels. The monobloc design gives the gun great strength, and simplifies the manufacturing process considerably. It is yet another example of how modern gunmakers make life easier for themselves while maintaining quality – and the benefits are passed on to the shooter in the form of lower prices.

While on the subject of over-and-under manufacture, it is interesting to note that, contrary to popular belief, some of the companies involved have a long and distinguished history. The Beretta family, for example, can trace their gunmaking story back no less than twelve generations, to Bartolomeo Beretta who lived from 1490 to 1567. Even Purdey's, the famous London makers, produce a small number of over-and-unders each year.

Pros and cons

The over-and-under's design inevitably means that it is less suitable for game shooting than the traditional side-by-side. Shooters who have come into the sport by way of clay pigeon shooting often prefer to use the type of gun with which they learnt to shoot, however, believing that they shoot more accurately with an over-and-under. They understand the drawbacks, and decide that they are outweighed by the advantages of using a familiar gun. There is nothing wrong with this, and I often use an over-and-under for rough shooting myself.

The disadvantages are not particularly serious in any case. You have to open an over-and-under to a relatively wide angle in order to eject the fired cases and reload, which may slow down your rate of fire marginally. This is completely irrelevant to the clay shooter, of course. Over-and-unders tend to be heavier than comparable side-by-sides, partly because of the design and partly because they are built that way for competitive clay shooting, which involves firing a large number of shots in a short space of time. A light gun would recoil more than the average shooter could accept in such circumstances. On top of all this, there is the illogical prejudice against over-and-unders that I mentioned in the previous chapter.

Many shooters who cut their teeth on an over-and-under would not dream of changing to a side-by-side for live game. The traditional double would feel unnatural in their hands, and they would shoot less well as a result. A well known East Anglian clay and game shooter once told me that he would much prefer to do all his shooting – driven pheasants included – with an over-and-under, despite having learned to shoot with a side-by-side. Indeed, he often took his Beretta over-and-under to formal game shoots. He admitted that the gun aroused comment, however, and said that he reverted to his Black Sable side-by-side in the most select company.

Clay pigeon shooting is very different from any form of rough or game shooting, despite having evolved as a form of practice for live shooting. This means that features of a gun which may be disadvantageous for one may be a positive advantage for the other. The weight of the average over-and-under would be impractical for a day walking-up grouse, for example, but it is very welcome when a Trap shooter finds himself firing two hundred cartridges in a couple of days – particularly when a single missed target can mean the difference between winning and losing. Top-level clay shooting demands intense concentration for hours at a time, and anything which reduces the recoil without lessening the gun's effectiveness is an advantage. With little distance to walk from one stand to the next, there is no reason not to have a gun as heavy as you can still swing easily.

The fore-end of an over-and-under wraps well round the barrels, protecting the shooter's hand from the heat produced by multiple shots. This is also true of repeaters, of course, and of the beavertail fore-ends fitted to some side-by-sides, but the splinter fore-end of the traditional side-by-side does not give this protection.

One of the most often quoted advantages of the over-and-under is the so-called 'single sighting plane', meaning that the shooter looks along a single barrel instead of two. The lower barrel is hidden from view beneath the rib and top barrel, and does not intrude into the view of the target. The argument is that you can see more of the target, or more of the space around it, than you would if your view was partially obscured by the double barrels of a side-by-side.

Many over-and-unders, particularly those intended for competitive Trap shooting, take this a step further by having a raised top rib. In theory, this should not make a great deal of difference if you shoot according to the textbooks, with both eyes open. In practice, however, many people reckon that the narrower sighting place of an over-and-under is more precise. Personally, I find that it encourages me to aim each shot more carefully. This improves my shooting on longer birds, but slows me down in instinctive, snap shots such as fast driven partridge clay targets.

9. Using an over-and-under for informal clay pigeon shooting.

Another feature of over-and-unders that makes them more suited to competitive clay shooting is the reduced muzzle flip on firing the lower barrel, which is normally fired first. This is more directly in line with the centre of the butt than on a similar side-by-side, and the recoil is taken more squarely on the shoulder. The muzzles tend not to jump so much with the shot, and you can fire a second, well-aimed shot more quickly. This is particularly important in Trap shooting, where an accurate second shot must be taken rapidly before the target flies out of range. Game shooters are less bothered by muzzle flip, partly because a miss is not so important since no-one is keeping the score, and partly because in game shooting you tend to take the gun from your shoulder between shots anyway.

This is typical of the difference in attitudes between clay and game shooters. A game shooter hopes that he will bring down the target, but with every shot different from the next he is not surprised – or even very upset – if he misses. Game shooting is an unpredictable sport, and there are many reasons for a miss that the shooter can console himself with. There are no prizes for the shooter who bags more than his neighbour, and therefore no incentive to pursue technicalities to the limit. Provided he can kill a reasonable percentage of what he shoots at, and, by killing the quarry cleanly, avoid inflicting unnecessary suffering, then a game shooter will be happy with his gun and hardly give it a second thought.

This is certainly not true of competitive clay shooters, who study the technical aspects of their sport very closely – sometimes too closely. In their efforts to kill the elusive last few targets, they can become obsessed with theories and measurements, and lose sight of the most important factor – the human element.

Clay shooters' attitudes are reflected in the enormous range of over-and-under shotguns available. There are models designed specif-

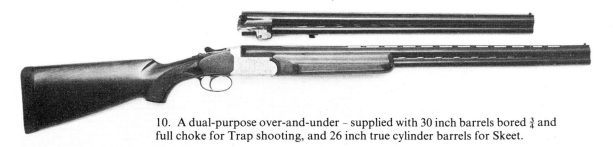

10. A dual-purpose over-and-under – supplied with 30 inch barrels bored ¾ and full choke for Trap shooting, and 26 inch true cylinder barrels for Skeet.

ically for each of the specialised disciplines – Trap, Skeet and Sporting – and within each of these there are many sub-divisions. A Trap gun, for example, may be designed for Down-the-Line, Automatic Ball Trap, or Universal Trench and Olympic Trap. It may have special features such as a Monte Carlo stock, and the barrels may be anything from 28 inches to 34 inches in length. Even the rib may be offered in various widths and finishes to suit individual styles and preferences. All this choice can be very confusing, but it does mean that you stand a good chance of finding an over-and-under that suits you well off-the-shelf, without having to have a gun specially made to fit.

A large number of different makes of over-and-under compete for a share of the market, with the result that these guns normally offer good value for money. It is worth studying the advertisements in the shooting press once you have decided on the gun you want, as many dealers offer good discounts, particularly on the more popular models. In fact, there are many of the 'old school' gunmakers who see this as a disturbing trend. They feel that the discount and mail order dealers are undercutting the traditional high street gunshops, and will eventually put them out of business. This would mean that a shooter would not be able to obtain the old fashioned advice and service that is now available.

Most over-and-unders have a single trigger, and the mechanism automatically switches to the second barrel when you fire the first. This saves you having to move your finger from one trigger to the next after the first shot as you do with a conventional side-by-side, allowing a quicker second shot. It also makes shooting with a pistol grip more convenient. Once again, this is more important to the clay shooter than the game or rough shooter. The single trigger mechanism may be operated by recoil, in which case a misfire prevents you from firing the second barrel without moving the barrel selector – which is normally located on the safety catch or in the upper part of the trigger blade. Some single trigger mechanisms are mechanical, in which case you can fire the second barrel by pulling the trigger again, even after a misfire.

Writing about misfires brings me to the subject of reliability. Clay shooters clearly cannot accept a gun that is not reliable. The rules allow a second attempt at a target if the gun misfires, but the shooter's concentration is broken and it is rare indeed for a competitor to shoot his best after a misfire. Gun failure is disastrous when every target counts, and over-and-unders would never have become so popular

23

with clay shooters if they were not reliable. This is one of the main reasons why repeaters have never really caught on with Britain's clay shooters, incidentally. When you consider that many clay shooters fire several hundred or even thousand cartridges in a season, it is obvious that modern over-and-unders can withstand heavy use.

In fact, over-and-unders are very strongly built, and their extra weight compared to a side-by-side allows the manufacturer to use thicker metal in the action and barrels. The average over-and-under will withstand pressures far higher than those encountered in normal British Proof testing, and identical guns destined for America, for instance, are proofed at higher levels as a matter of course. This is relatively unimportant to the average user, who will never want to shoot more powerful cartridges anyway, but it is comforting to know that the gun has a considerable margin of strength.

Modern over-and-unders have reached an extraordinary level of development, and this trend continues as manufacturers strive to cater for every whim and fancy among clay shooters. A cynic might say that manufacturers go to the lengths of creating or at least encouraging such trends themselves in order to stimulate sales. It is certainly true that, immediately a gun with some unusual feature is used to win a major event, many lesser shots are tempted to try the same thing in the hope that it may help them to improve.

Consider the example of the Perazzi DB81E. Intended for Olympic Trap shooting, this very specialised over-and-under has a high floating rib which stands over half an inch above the top barrel. The barrels have a series of vents between them, so that air can flow through and dissipate heat more quickly. The stock is of the Monte Carlo type, with the comb parallel to the line of the barrels. This allows you to place your cheek at any point along its length without affecting the relationship of eye to rib, and also to adopt a more head-up position.

The coil mainsprings in the action are made of special steel, tempered to give the fastest possible lock time – the time taken for the hammer to fall and ignite the cartridge once the trigger is pulled. Perazzi, like a few other manufacturers, have also developed a 'release' trigger for competition guns, which fires when you release the pressure on the trigger blade rather than pulling. The idea is to help the shooter to relax his muscles instead of tightening up as he fires. The system takes some getting used to, but some top competitors swear by it.

All these refinements have come about because clay shooters are prepared to pay for anything that may improve their scores. Some of them make little or no practical difference, but you want all the help you can get when a single point can be all that stands between you and an Olympic medal. Confidence in your equipment is vital at any level of competition, and the psychological element is not to be ignored. A feature that you believe confers an advantage may do just that – for the simple reason that you have faith in it.

Some time ago, a company called Sussex Armoury went into liquidation. At the time they were importing the Rizzini range of over-and-unders from Italy. In the subsequent sale of stock, many of these guns were knocked down for bargain prices. I bought a Trap model, my first over-and-under, with the intention of using it for clay pigeons and a certain amount of rough shooting. It seemed a good choice as an all-round gun, since I had found that the long barrels and high comb of a Trap gun suited me well. My arms are fairly long, and swinging the gun proved to be no problem   yet the 30-inch barrels prevented me stopping my swing at the vital moment.

The only problem with the gun as an all-round weapon was the chokes, which were rather tight since the gun was intended for long-

11. This modestly priced over-and-under has attractive engraving on the action. It is slightly unusual in having two triggers – many over-and-unders have a single selective trigger.

range Trap targets. On the advice of Chris Cradock, I had the gun fitted with screw-in choke tubes made by Nigel Teague. Since then I have used it for almost every kind of shooting imaginable, and it has performed extremely well. Almost the only situation where it would be patently out of place is at a formal driven game shoot, where its slightly slower reloading and the fact that it is an over-and-under would make it less suitable than a traditional side-by-side. I have also carried the Rizzini for many miles across Highland grouse moors, which proved to me that it is really too heavy for this type of shooting. Nevertheless, it would be hard to beat as an all-round weapon for a shooter who is unlikely to find himself invited to a formal shoot, or walking many miles in search of his quarry. For a specialised gun, it has proved to be remarkably versatile.

On the subject of versatility, you will probably realise by now that I do not believe that there is such a thing as an 'all-round' gun. In my opinion, the side-by-side is ideal for game shooting, and an over-and-under cannot be beaten for clays. Either type will perform more than adequately at both, however, and I certainly would not turn down an invitation to shoot driven pheasants because I only had an over-and-under.

3 The pump-action repeater

The pump-action shotgun is rarely seen in Britain, although it has long been a favourite of American hunters. Pump-actions are as American as apple pie, in fact. They were developed as a relatively cheap, rugged tool to meet the needs of the American market gunners, and have never really become popular on this side of the Atlantic.

Nowadays one can buy high grade pump-actions from makers such as Weatherby and Browning, but this type of shotgun is still bought largely as a shooting machine rather than as a thing of inherent beauty. Pump-actions do have a certain functional beauty of their own, however, but this is not comparable to that of a 'best' English side-by-side. Indeed, it would be unfair to draw such a comparison. The two fulfil totally different roles, and one of the few things that they have in common is that they use the same ammunition.

The mechanism
Pump-action shotguns were developed from slide-action repeating rifles, and follow the same principles of design. The cartridges are loaded into a magazine tube which is located below the single barrel. Sliding the fore-end backwards and forwards operates the action, ejecting the fired cartridge case from the chamber and loading a fresh shell from the magazine. At the same time, the hammer is cocked so that simply pulling the trigger will fire the next round. A locking mechanism prevents the action from opening until the shell has been fired, or the release catch is depressed.

The mechanism consists basically of a breech block contained within the receiver, which is connected to the fore-end by a single or double action bar. Pulling back on the fore-end unlocks the breech block and moves it rearwards within the receiver, and spring-loaded claws grip the cartridge case head – extracting it from the chamber. At the full extent of the rearward stroke, a fixed stud knocks the case sideways, freeing it from the extractor claws and throwing it out of the ejection port in the side of the receiver. The next cartridge is released from the magazine, and is raised by a lever-operated platform into line with the breech opening as the breech block moves forwards again, pushing it into the chamber. As the breech block reaches its most forward position, the locking mechanism fixes it firmly in place so that it cannot be blown back by the cartridge when you fire.

This description of the pump-action mechanism makes it clear that there is more to go wrong in these guns than in a conventional break-barrel design. Breakdowns and jams do happen, but modern pump-actions have been developed to reduce these to a minimum. Most of the problems that I have experienced with these guns have been my own fault, usually caused by my failing to bring the fore-end back fully to the end of its stroke. If you do this, the fresh cartridge is released before the old case is ejected, and the two jam together in the receiver. This is the result of changing from pump-action to break-barrel and back. If I used a pump-action more regularly, the problem would not occur.

The action of sliding the fore-end back and forth sounds complicated and distracting to those who have never tried a pump-action gun, but it soon becomes second nature provided you do not swap from one type of gun to another too frequently. In fact, some advocates of the pump-action say that sliding the fore-end to and fro helps you to swing more positively onto the target for a second shot, and counteracts any tendency for the muzzle to jump out of alignment on firing.

With practice, you can fire repeated, well aimed shots from a pump-action remarkably quickly. I used to place a tin can at a distance of a few yards in front of me, and empty a five-shot magazine at it in a matter of seconds. The idea was to knock the can as far as possible

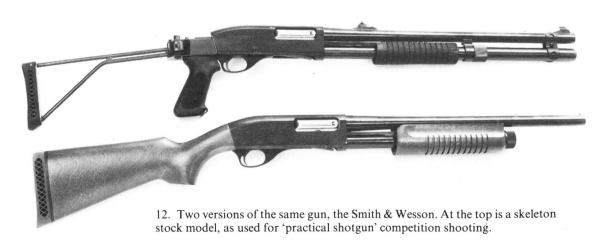

12. Two versions of the same gun, the Smith & Wesson. At the top is a skeleton stock model, as used for 'practical shotgun' competition shooting.

without letting it come to rest before being hit by the next shot. This is nothing compared to the feats performed by some of the old trick shooters such as Carver, who would shoot blocks of wood that he threw into the air himself – emptying the magazine before the first block touched the ground.

A small number of clay pigeon shooters have used pump-action guns with great success, which must surely refute the argument that they are unwieldy and difficult to handle effectively. To a shooter who is familiar with more traditional weapons, the pump-action certainly feels very strange, and working the action is likely to distract him – but a little practice soon puts this right.

Advantages of the pump-action

Like all guns, the pump-action has advantages and disadvantages that make it more suitable for some forms of shooting and less so for others. Among the advantages, its single barrel gives a narrow sighting plane which is very pointable, similar to that of an over-and-under. It also keeps its own supply of cartridges ready for use and protected in the magazine tube from damp and dirt. This is very helpful to the wildfowler, for example, who may fumble with cold, gloved hands and drop his fresh shells in the mud.

Another advantage of the pump-action is that it is relatively cheap to produce. Made mainly from pressed steel and fairly roughly machined parts, it is assembled on a production line system which turns out the guns in large numbers. This makes pump actions relatively inexpensive, well suited to the shooter who does not want to spend a great deal of money on a gun, yet requires the ability to fire repeated shots.

The 'advantage' of being able to fire five or more shots in quick succession is really no advantage at all to the average sportsman. Certainly, no sportsman worthy of the name would fire more than a couple of shots at a single bird, or even a covey of birds. Usually, there is only time for two or at the most three shots at a bird before it flies out of range, in any case. I do not believe that many users of repeaters misuse them in this way, however, whatever some opponents of them may say. The users of this type of gun that I have met are well aware of their responsibilities to the quarry, and they are equally well aware that others eye them with suspicion. If anything, they will take pains to display an even higher level of sportsmanship than their fellows with break-barrel guns, and their behaviour is normally beyond reproach. It is also worth noting that having a spare round available in the magazine can sometimes allow a 'mercy' shot to finish off a wounded bird that might otherwise take a few minutes to retrieve.

The Wildlife & Countryside Act requires that repeating shotguns must be fitted with a magazine plug that restricts their capacity to two shots in the magazine and one in the breech for certain species of quarry – basically those species normally regarded as game as opposed to vermin. Refer to Appendix I for details of this and other aspects of the law relating to shotguns.

One role in which the multi-shot capacity of repeaters is undeniably valuable is that of 'law enforcement' as the Americans are inclined to call it – rather euphemistically, I feel. Special models of the more popular makes of pump-action are available for this purpose. They are widely used in the States by the Police, and have also been chosen for specialised uses by the armed forces. The shotgun, with its wide spread of shot and easy pointability, is well suited to close range combat. Loaded with buckshot and fitted with a shortened barrel and special stock, the pump-action in particular is an ideal weapon for fighting at close quarters in enclosed areas such as buildings. This type of gun is also popular with 'practical shotgun' enthusiasts, who compete over a

13. A short-barrelled Mossberg pump-action, with rifle style sights. This gun is intended for firing solid slug ammunition, and is bored true cylinder.

course of targets simulating human enemies in 'realistic' situations. Extra realism is added by 'good guy' targets which represent hostages or innocent bystanders, and score penalty points if hit. This sport developed from practical pistol shooting, and is growing rapidly in the United Kingdom – particularly in the South East. Certain gunshops specialise in supplying riot control type pump-action shotguns, and conversion kits for the standard 'sporting' models.

The pump-action is also well suited to firing solid projectiles such as the Brenneke slug. The barrel can be fitted with rifle-type sights to give sufficient accuracy to kill deer and other large animals at ranges up to seventy-five or even one hundred yards. This type of ammunition is rarely used in Britain, largely due to the fact that it requires a Firearms Certificate, but it is popular in America, where the shotgun and slug ammunition is sometimes known as the 'poor man's rifle'.

Disadvantages
One of the major disadvantages of the pump-action is that in almost any company the user is regarded as a 'cowboy'. It tends therefore to be the weapon of solitary shooters, such as wildfowlers and rough shooters. It also has the disadvantage of being awkward to dismantle for cleaning and transport, and the shape is not particularly good for carrying over rough ground. In particular, the loading slot in the underside of the action makes it quite painful to carry in the crook of your arm, as you would a side-by-side. A sling or sleeve is the best means of carrying a pump-action to the spot where you intend to shoot.

The pump-action's receiver makes it longer than a comparable break-barrel gun by some 4 to 5 inches (10 to 12.5 centimetres). I find that this can help it to point well, but it can be a drawback if you use a pump-action in a confined space – a pigeon hide for example. Because the barrel is fixed, it is not easy to check that the bore is free of obstructions when you load. I generally open the action and then look down the muzzle end, but you must take extra care when using a pump-action in snow or muddy conditions. A blockage could cause the gun to burst, with lethal results.

Similarly, making the gun safe before crossing a fence or other obstacle is more complicated with a pump-action than with traditional weapons. Opening the action, which entails depressing the release catch, will free the next shell in the magazine, and if you attempt to close it again the gun will jam. You must remove one of the shells from the action before closing the mechanism, and then replace the second shell in the magazine via the loading port. A few pump-action shotguns have a magazine stop catch to avoid this.

The magazine system also means that you cannot give yourself the option of different types of cartridge in the gun at once, at least not without becoming totally confused. With a side-by-side or over-and-under, you can load, say, 1 ounce (30 gramme) cartridges in one barrel and $1\frac{1}{8}$ ounce (34 gramme) shells in the other. Loading one behind the other in the magazine of a pump-action is possible, but it is all too easy to lose track of the sequence. This is not often a serious problem, but there have been occasions when, for instance, I have wanted to load a heavy BB cartridge in the choke barrel in case a fox appears as I patrol the rearing pen in summer.

The pump-action is not as prone to malfunction as some people believe – a misconception which is probably fostered by the gun's tendency to jam if not handled positively. But it is true that these guns do go wrong from time to time. Even in this case, the cause is probably not entirely the gun. Swollen or unsuitable cartridges, or debris in the mechanism, can cause a jam, for instance. Whatever the cause, a jammed mechanism is a nuisance – and in the case of a police marksman it could cost him his life.

One problem is that some pump-action mechanisms tend to be somewhat fussy about cartridges, and will cause trouble with certain brands. In general, American shells work best in American-made pump-actions – or so I have found. I once owned a very cheap pump-action which had a definite dislike of British cartridges, and eventually refused to extract and eject fired cases of any make. It turned out that the chamber was slightly over-size, and the cartridge heads were expanding too much and sticking. This put too much strain on the extractor claw, which was not very well designed in the first place. Finally, I decided to return the gun to the dealer, who to his credit

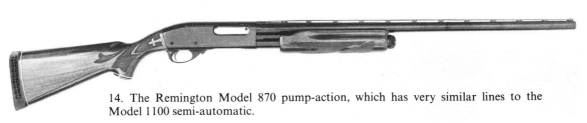

14. The Remington Model 870 pump-action, which has very similar lines to the Model 1100 semi-automatic.

refunded my money in full without a murmur of argument.

The pump-action's single barrel, as opposed to the two of a side-by-side or over-and-under, can be an advantage or a disadvantage, depending on the circumstances. It means that a variable choke device can be fitted more cheaply and simply, and also makes the gun potentially more accurate with slugs. But a blockage or dent can put a stop to the day's shooting when a double barrelled gun could continue.

Another disadvantage of the pump-action, to my mind, is the noise of operating the mechanism. There are few occasions when this actually affects the bag, although I once lost the opportunity of shooting a fox when it heard the action shut. I should point out, incidentally, that I would not dream of shooting a fox in hunting country; the creature in question was causing serious damage on a Scottish island where there was no other means of controlling foxes humanely. Returning to my argument, my real objection is that the crash-bang-wallop of reloading a pump-action seems unnecessarily crude, and strangely out of place on the shoot. I say strangely because the noise is nothing compared to the boom of a shot, but it has a harsh metallic quality that lacks the preciseness of a side-by-side or over-and-under.

Nevertheless, there will always be a place in my gun cupboard for a pump-action, if only as a knockabout tool for those occasions when I would be fearful of damaging a more valuable weapon. Ferreting is a good example, when, laden down with ferret box, spade, game bag and so on, it is very easy to give the gun a knock. I also tend to use a pump-action when I am shooting in adverse conditions such as wildfowling – for much the same reason. If damage to the gun seems likely, I would far rather risk a pump-action than my treasured side-by-side.

15. The Winchester Ranger pump-action shotgun, fitted with the manufacturer's 'Winchoke' screw-in choke tube system.

4 The semi-automatic

Automatic is the name given to those shotguns that reload themselves from a magazine on firing. In fact, 'semi-automatic' would be a more accurate description, since a true automatic would continue firing until you released the trigger, or until the supply of fresh rounds in the magazine was exhausted. The term automatic is generally used by shotgun shooters, however, and having pointed out the inaccuracy, I shall use this description.

Automatic mechanisms
There are several different automatic mechanisms, although all of them perform the same basic function. They are essentially similar to the pump-action mechanism, except that the force required to operate them comes from the discharge of the previous cartridge rather than being supplied by the shooter.

In some types of automatic shotgun, this force comes from the recoil of the barrel and breech assembly. These recoil-operated automatics fall into two categories – long recoil and short recoil.

The long recoil system was developed by John Moses Browning at the beginning of the twentieth century. In guns of this type, the barrel and breech block lock together, and the recoil forces them back together by about 3 inches (7.5 centimetres). At the end of their travel, the breech block is caught by a sear, while the barrel is returned to the forward position by spring pressure. This frees the fired case, which is ejected, making way for the next shell. The sear then releases the breech block, which flies forward again, pushing the fresh cartridge into the chamber. In moving backwards, the breech block also cocks the hammer, so the gun is ready to fire again when the trigger is pulled.

In the short recoil system, the barrel is fixed, and a separate chamber block moves back a fraction of an inch, giving the breech block enough of a kick to throw it backwards, eject the fired case, cock the hammer and load the next cartridge.

This is almost a gas-operated system, in that the chamber block is forced backwards largely by gas pressure, but the true gas-operated automatic works on an entirely different principle. The chamber and barrel are in one piece, and fixed firmly to the receiver. A piston housed beneath the barrel is moved rearwards in its cylinder by compressed gases which pass through a hole in the barrel wall. The gas obviously cannot find its way to the piston cylinder until after the shot and wadding have passed the gas port. As the piston moves back, it unlocks the breech block, pushes it rearwards, and operates the action as before – ejecting the fired case, cocking the hammer, and loading another cartridge from the magazine into the chamber. The delay between the piston starting to move and the action actually opening ensures that the shot has left the muzzle before the breech opens.

One problem that faces designers of gas operated automatics is the variety of cartridges available, not to mention those produced by home loading enthusiasts. The pressure exerted on the piston must be sufficient to operate the action, but too much gas at too high a pressure would cause problems. If the shooter is going to use various loads, with their different pressure characteristics, then there must be some means of adjusting the mechanism's sensitivity. This is sometimes achieved by varying the size of the gas port or ports, by moving a load selector to a 'high' or 'low' setting. Other mechanisms react to different cartridges by automatically metering the amount of gas tapped from the barrel, and adjusting themselves accordingly.

Manufacture
As with pump-actions, few shooters buy an automatic for its looks or fine balance. More often, they want a relatively cheap gun that will do the job with the minimum of fuss. Most makers of automatics or pump-actions, for that matter – concentrate on keeping frills and embellishments to the minimum. They produce their guns as cheaply as possible without reducing their efficiency, since they must sell into a very competitive market.

As a result, many automatics are fairly basic pieces of equipment, with plain stocks, indifferent wood-to-metal fit, and a minimum of engraving and other attention to detail. Their designers attach great importance to ease and economy of manufacture as well as to function. Every part of the gun is machined as little as possible; not a hole is drilled or a bend made without a good reason, because every extra operation costs money.

There are exceptions, of course. Like all types of gun, automatics have their fans, or fanatics, and manufacturers produce high grade guns to suit them. These are decorated with good quality engraving, have specially selected walnut stocks that are chequered and finished to a high standard, and receive the kind of attention that is generally reserved for the better grades of side-by-side or over-and-under. The internal parts of these weapons are the same as in the cheaper models, but they receive extra polishing and fitting to achieve a smoother operation. Such guns are very much the exceptions to the rule, however, and represent a tiny fraction of the number of automatics sold.

Pros and cons of the automatic

It is characteristic of all automatic shotguns that they recoil less than other weapons of the same weight firing the same ammunition. This is a result of the mechanism moving back and forth, partly compensating for and absorbing the recoil. For this reason, automatics are often recommended to beginners and ladies. Not that they are any less suitable for the more experienced shooter. Many top clay shots use an automatic for all or some of their shooting, and Duncan Lawton, for instance, has won dozens of championships up to World level with a Remington 1100 automatic. The reduced recoil makes long events less punishing, and allows a quick, well aimed second shot.

The recoil of an automatic feels entirely different to that of a conventional gun in other ways, too. The sensation is more like a double recoil, since you can feel two distinct nudges in the shoulder – the first as the cartridge fires and pushes back against the locked breech block, and the second when the breech block reaches the end of its travel and reverses direction. This can be quite unnerving when you fire an automatic for the first time, particularly as the fired case flies out of the ejection port in the side of the receiver in full view of your aiming eye. Although this is distracting to begin with, one soon becomes accustomed to it – and it certainly does not seem to bother shooters who are experienced with automatics.

In most other ways, the advantages and disadvantages of automatics

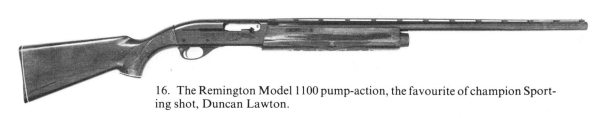

16. The Remington Model 1100 pump-action, the favourite of champion Sporting shot, Duncan Lawton.

are much the same as those of pump-actions. Their design and operation are very similar, except that an automatic reloads itself after every shot whereas the shooter must operate the pump-action's mechanism. The firepower of an automatic is deceptive. Certainly, even an inexperienced shooter can empty the magazine remarkably quickly, even when taking aimed shots. But refilling the magazine is relatively slow, even with guns such as the Remington 1100 which is designed for rapid reloading. With this gun, the breech remains open after the last shot in the magazine. You place the first cartridge in the ejection port, and turn the gun upside down to insert the remaining shells in the magazine. The action of touching the loading lever releases the breech block, closing the action without the need to press a separate release catch.

Even this does not speed up the loading process sufficiently to give the automatic a capacity for sustained firepower that equals a pair of side-by-sides with a loader. This is definitely not why automatics are such a rare sight on game shoots. Once again, the real reason is illogical prejudice – stronger, if anything, than against pump-actions.

Outside the clay pigeon shooting field, automatics are well suited to sport where the opportunity arises for repeated shots at infrequent intervals. Pigeon shooting is one example, where a flock of pigeons may come in to the decoys and present a chance for four or five shots. The birds are unlikely to return for some time, giving the shooter the opportunity he needs to reload the magazine. And since pigeon are pests, the shooter need not feel guilty about taking more than a couple of birds from a flock.

I have met shooters with automatics in all kinds of situations from grouse shooting to vermin control, but the vast majority of automatics in this country are used for clay shooting. Even so, they pose no real threat to the superiority of the over-and-under in this field. Some people particularly like the low recoil of the automatic and find that this, combined with the narrow sighting plane and modest price, gives the automatic the edge. Their popularity as a beginner's weapon ensures that a good number of shooters cut their teeth on one, and decide to stay with the familiar design when they progress beyond the novice stage. Brought up on an automatic, they find the recoil of a conventional weapon excessive, and are reluctant to make the change.

One personal grumble of mine, which applies equally to all mass-produced repeaters, is that the stock measurements seem to bear little relation to those of the average shooter (if such a creature exists). In

37

general, automatics and pumps seem to have abnormally short stocks with a pronounced drop to the comb. This means that shooters of average build, particularly if they are used to shooting with a side-by-side or over-and-under, must adapt their style to suit the gun. The alternative is to alter the stock, which can be difficult. Adding to the stock's length is simple enough, although the results may not be pretty, and it should be possible with a little ingenuity to make a comb raiser. But cast-off is virtually impossible to achieve when the action and stock bolt protrude into the hand of the stock itself.

I added a spacer and comb raiser to one of my guns, making the length and comb height almost identical to those of my professionally fitted side-by-side. While I can now bring the gun more easily up to the aim, I must make a conscious effort to tilt my head sideways in order to place my cheek firmly on the comb. If I do not, I miss the target above and slightly to the left. This is only a relatively minor problem, however, and one that I would soon overcome if I used the gun exclusively.

Another criticism that is often levelled at automatics is their tendency to jam and break down. Few users of automatics would deny that they do fail occasionally, and probably more often than break-barrel weapons. The complexity of the automatic mechanism means that there are more working parts that can go wrong, and more nooks and crevices in which debris can lodge. The automatic's receiver, with its loading aperture and ejection port, gives only partial protection against dirt and pieces of twig and leaf, and it is far easier for the works to foul up than with a side-by-side or over-and-under in which the most delicate parts are more fully enclosed.

Nevertheless, automatics are generally quite simple to strip down and clean, and regular maintenance will virtually eliminate malfunctions. Problems arise when the shooter expects to use his gun week after week, giving it no more than a squirt of oil and a quick rub with a cloth.

As proof that automatics can be reliable, they have been chosen by people whose lives depend on them. Soldiers in the trenches and the jungles of Malaya, for instance, have used automatic shotguns as a short-range weapon, and some United States police forces rely on them for 'riot control' and 'law enforcement' duties. If you study the photographs of the Iranian Embassy siege of a few years ago, you will also see that the automatic has its admirers among the SAS.

5 Special purpose guns

The drilling

The drilling is, quite simply, a combined shotgun and rifle. It normally has two smooth-bored barrels arranged as a conventional side-by-side, with the third, rifled barrel situated between and slightly below the other two. This third barrel replaces the bottom rib of the normal side-by-side.

Other variations on the same theme may have a single smooth-bored barrel and a rifled barrel, arranged one above the other like an over-and-under. This type is sometimes based on a standard over-and-under action, in fact, whereas the first type has to be specially built from scratch.

The drilling is rare in the United Kingdom, where it would require a Firearms Certificate which would restrict the shooter to using it in specified places. However, the real reason for its rarity here is that there is little call for such a gun. Few shooters would have cause to use a drilling more than once or twice a year – yet they would be carrying the weight of an extra barrel all the time.

The drilling is a compromise, and at best can perform little more than adequately as a shotgun and as a rifle. As a shotgun, it will be rather heavier and more unwieldy than a comparable side-by-side. Its loading gape will be wider than normal, too.

As a rifle, it will be much less comfortable to aim than a gun designed specially for shooting stationary targets, and it is unlikely to have provision for fitting a telescopic sight. If it does, the mounting block will spoil the shooter's line of sight when he swings onto a moving target.

The drilling is much more popular on the Continent, however, where it is used whenever dangerous medium-sized game may be encountered – wild boar, for example. It is easy to see why a shooter, faced with the prospect of meeting an enraged boar at close quarters, might prefer to carry a gun with greater firepower than would be considered normal in this country. As a result, the few drillings that are seen in this country are normally in the hands of visiting continentals. They are

17. The author's folding single-barrel hammer .410 shotgun – almost guaranteed to give the user a reputation as a poacher!

18. An example of the drilling, a side-by-side shotgun with a rifled barrel in place of the bottom rib. Note the rifle-style open sights on the top rib.

generally engraved in the heavy, florid Germanic style – often with boar shooting scenes.

Those shooters who wish to use their shotguns on larger than normal quarry in this country often take the simpler option of acquiring solid slug ammunition. This is available in all the more common gauges, and rifled slugs such as the Brenneke are capable of surprising accuracy at short to medium ranges. Such ammunition may not be obtained or used in the United Kingdom without a Firearms Certificate.

The bolt-action
The bolt-action mechanism is more often associated with rifles than with shotguns, but there are a variety of bolt-action shotguns available. These tend to be in the more extreme bore sizes – notably .410 and 10 bore. However, bolt-action 12 bores are not unknown. Bolt-action is

41

also the preferred design for the very small calibre smoothbore guns known as 'garden guns', such as the 9mm.

The main advantages of the bolt-action are its strength and its simplicity. The barrel and action body can be firmly jointed, without the need for a hinge, and the bolt slides to and fro in a simple tube. Twisting the bolt through ninety degrees or so locks it firmly shut, and the extractor claws grip the fired case to remove it from the chamber. In the more usual form of bolt-action weapon, the next cartridge is fed from a magazine in front of the trigger guard, and you load it simply by closing the bolt. This can be done relatively quickly, but it prevents you from taking fast double shots because you have to release your grip on the stock in order to operate the bolt.

Nevertheless, the bolt-action has a place as a rugged tool for pest destruction by someone who will spend little time on care and maintenance. It also has its advantages in harsh conditions, such as on the marsh, where a more delicate weapon might become clogged with dirt and debris.

Marlin produce a bolt-action magnum shotgun for goose shooting, in 10 and 12 bore magnum gauges. This is a monster of a weapon, with a barrel no less than a yard long. The gun looks so strong and heavy that it is difficult to imagine how anyone could even carry it onto the marsh, let along swing onto a fast moving target in dim light. But I once handled one of these weapons on the Parker-Hale stand at a Game Fair, and I was surprised to find that it mounted and swung like a much smaller, conventionally balanced weapon.

It is open to doubt whether the long barrel of these guns actually provides any advantage in terms of range or pattern quality. More likely the length is there because the manufacturer believes that potential buyers of the weapon think a long barrel shoots further and

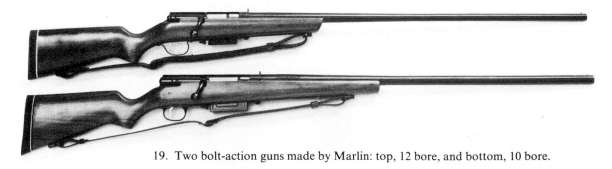

19. Two bolt-action guns made by Marlin: top, 12 bore, and bottom, 10 bore.

harder. This belief has carried over from the days of black powder, when a long barrel made more efficient use of the powder charge and produced truly superior results.

The bolt-action, then, has its place in the world of shotgun shooting, although the mechanism is more obviously suited to rifle shooting, where slowness of loading is more in keeping with the tempo of the sport. Many shotgunners will have learned to shoot with an old Webley bolt-action .410, and will consequently have a special fondness for this design.

The Martini-action
Like the bolt-action, the Martini action is more commonly associated with rifles. This design was chosen for the Martini Henry service rifle, largely for its strength and reliability, although it has long since been superseded by more modern weapons. Variations on the Martini Henry design are still used by target shooters, however.

The Martini action consists of a heavy, solid breech block which is pivoted at the rearmost end. It is opened by operating the lever below the trigger guard. Pulling the lever downwards allows the breech block to drop, exposing the open breech and at the same time ejecting the fired cartridge case up and backwards.

The shooter inserts the next cartridge by hand, and closes the breech by operating the lever. This type of weapon frequently has a large, positive safety catch in the form of a thumb lever on the side of the action.

The Webley Greener GP is the classic example of this mechanism applied to a shotgun. First designed by the almost legendary W. W. Greener at the turn of the century, it was based on the Martini Henry rifle and has hardly changed since. The Greener GP was never intended to compete on equal terms with side-by-side or over-and-under shotguns, even in their lowest grades. It is meant as a 'knockabout' gun for farmers, explorers and anyone else who is unlikely to spend a great deal of time and trouble in looking after his gun, but will expect it to perform faultlessly when necessary. As such, it could hardly be bettered. Very few guns would survive the abuse that the Greener GP will take in its stride. I remember W. & C. Scott's John Knight proudly telling me of the terrible things that previous owners had done to their Greener GPs – which had continued to work as though nothing had happened. He also informed me that the guns were still in great

43

demand from overseas, and W. & C. Scott make around seven hundred a year.

Despite the somewhat clumsy appearance of these guns, they are quite light and easy to handle. They come to the shoulder well, and swing naturally, with the weight nicely between the hands. The Martini mechanism is obviously slow to reload, and offers only a single shot, but experts have been known to load and fire a Greener GP fifteen times in one minute – or one shot every four seconds. This rate of fire would be difficult to keep up under field conditions, but the need would never arise. The Greener GP is a masterpiece of timeless, functional design, and it is a shame that many of these guns are doomed to spend their working lives rattling around the back of a Land-Rover or rusting forgotten in a tractor shed corner.

The punt gun

The punt gun has now virtually passed into folklore, kept alive by a tiny number of enthusiasts. The days are gone when men could make a living by hunting wildfowl with these massive, boat-borne guns. Those who use punt guns now follow the sport purely for the excitement and satisfaction of going back in time and battling single-handed against the sea and the quarry.

The punt gun is one of the simplest forms of shotgun devised. It consists of a huge, gas pipe of a barrel, and a breech piece which is screwed or bolted to one end. The firing mechanism is most often a hammer action lock similar to those on early percussion muzzle loaders. There is no stock on the punt gun, since the gun is mounted on the punt, or boat, and is in any case far too heavy to be mounted, let alone

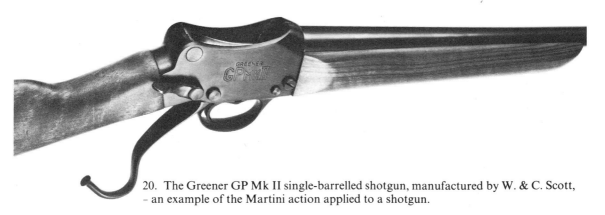

20. The Greener GP Mk II single-barrelled shotgun, manufactured by W. & C. Scott,
– an example of the Martini action applied to a shotgun.

fired in the shoulder. To fire the gun, you pull a cord or lanyard which is attached to the rudimentary trigger.

The punt gun's charge is normally made up in a rolled paper tube by the shooter himself, since no manufacturer would consider it economic to make the small number of cartridges that he could sell. There is little standardisation in punt guns anyway, and each gun requires ammunition of slightly different dimensions.

It is outside the scope of this book to describe the use of punt guns and the equipment that goes with them. A full explanation would fill a book in itself, and the subject is adequately covered in other works. Colonel Peter Hawker's classic *Instructions to Young Sportsmen* contains a fascinating chapter on the subject, and is well worth reading.

In essence, the gun is mounted on a punt – which is a boat shaped roughly like a canoe. The shooter lies on his stomach, and propels the boat with short paddles, or sticks if the water is shallow enough to reach the bottom. Using enormous skill and fieldcraft, not to mention endless patience, he manoeuvres the boat into range of a party of ducks on the water, firing when the charge of shot will bring down the maximum number of birds. The range may be anything up to 100 yards (100 metres) or so. The gunner then moves in with his 'cripple stopper' normally an old 12 bore shoulder gun.

The punt gun itself may have a bore of $1\frac{1}{2}$ inches ($3\frac{3}{4}$ centimetres) or even more in extreme cases, and will fire several ounces of shot. It must be mounted securely to the boat in order to prevent it recoiling back into the face of the shooter.

Although punt gunning as described above sounds little short of mass murder to those who have never tried it, the shooter may spend many days or even weeks before he manages to manoeuvre himself into a suitable position for a shot. When the time comes, he understandably feels entitled to take a number of birds with a single shot.

So far as I am aware, no gunsmith makes punt guns nowadays, and I would be surprised to find a single punt gun that had been made in the last fifty years. The few remaining enthusiasts keep their existing guns in working order and use them very occasionally, but it is a most unlucky duck that falls victim to one nowadays.

Multi-barrelled guns
Various gunsmiths in the past have tried to increase the firepower of their guns by giving them three, four or even more barrels. Such guns

45

certainly allowed the shooter to fire more shots before reloading, but the overall advantage is arguably slight. A multi-barrelled gun is inevitably heavier than its single or double barrelled counterpart, making it less convenient to carry and to shoot. Loading a multi-barrelled gun is also slower, so sustained firepower is not so great as might be imagined. The occasions when a chance arises to fire more than a couple of shots in quick succession are few and far between, too, as I mentioned in a previous chapter. Most sportsmen would happily miss the opportunity for a triple or quadruple kill, and save themselves the trouble of carrying a gun which in any case is likely to cause some leg pulling.

21. A rare sight nowadays – a gunning punt. The oar in the foreground is used to steer the punt.

Modern shooters who do feel the need for some back-up shots can choose from a wide range of modern repeating shotguns – pump-action or semi-automatic. Yet the multi-barrelled weapon does hold a certain fascination for shooters and gunmakers alike. To the gun-maker, it represents a unique challenge. It is difficult enough to make a double-barrelled gun that shoots to the point of aim with both barrels, and has a mechanism that works efficiently. A multi-barrelled gun poses much greater problems, and for this reason some gunsmiths are tempted to test their skill by making one.

One example of this was the Famar four-barrelled gun, which I saw at the 1982 Game Fair. It was a 28 bore, made as a prototype for a run of fifteen hand-made .410's. The gun had two external hammers, firing the top two barrels, and internal hammers for the bottom two. The external finish was immaculate, and I found the gun nicely balanced and comfortable to handle. It was a credit to the craftsman who made it, but I cannot see myself using one for serious shooting.

An air-powered shotgun

All the guns described so far in this book are powered by a charge of powder which is ignited and burns to produce the gas that drives the shot up the barrel. But this is not the only way of doing the job. It is possible to use compressed gas, which is released on pulling the trigger. The only example of an air-powered shotgun that I have ever seen was made by Daystate, a company that have made a name for themselves by producing tranquilliser guns, which are used in safari parks and the like to immobilise large, dangerous animals without harming them.

I learned that they had been asked to design a weapon for controlling small birds and rodents in food stores, where lead pellets were out of the question, and quiet operation would be a distinct advantage. Their answer was to adapt one of their compressed air tranquilliser gun mechanisms, powered by a cylinder of air contained in the fore-end. Fitted with a smoothbore barrel and a bolt action to accept shot cartridges, it would fire a small charge of hard sugar balls with enough force to kill small vermin at the relatively short ranges involved. The gun will also fire lead pellets, but its range and power fall well short of conventional 12 bore shotguns.

The Daystate air-powered shotgun is a functional weapon, designed for a specific purpose. It is not beautiful, nor is it finished to a high standard in the same way as a competition or game shotgun. It does

47

not handle like a normal shotgun, either, and it would be difficult to shoot well with it at conventional shotgun targets.

To me, it is the idea behind the gun that is its most interesting aspect. One of the most pressing problems faced by Britain's numerous small gun clubs is the complaints about 'noise pollution'. Local residents sometimes campaign to have clubs closed, or shooting restricted to once or twice a month, because of the noise every weekend. A compressed air shotgun is virtually silent in use, and if someone could only come up with one that was as effective and satisfying to use as a conventional 12 bore, then it could revolutionise clay shooting at club level. Compressed air shotguns are also very cheap to shoot, the only cost being the shot itself (once you have a means of compressing the air), and this could have a big impact on clay shooting.

I have a feeling that all this is just a pipe dream, however.

PART II

THEORY

22. A lesson from an experienced coach can be invaluable. The coach here is Michael Rose of West London Shooting School.

6 Technique, gun balance and handling

Every shooter has his own individual style of shooting, but the basic techniques are more or less the same. This is not particularly surprising, since the style or technique adopted by every shooter has the same purpose – to place the pattern on the target in flight in order to kill or break it.

This means that the gun must be pointing at the place where the target *will* be by the time the shot reaches it. The shooter must fire at a point in front of the target and along its projected line of flight, so that the pattern and the target arrive at the same point in space at the same time. The distance that you aim in front of the target is called the lead.

You could achieve the desired effect by aiming at a point ahead of the target with the gun stationary, firing at the precise moment to give the correct lead. This is a clumsy technique, generally known as 'poking'. It leaves the shooter wide open to errors of judgment, as well as variations in his reaction time from one day to the next (even from before lunch to after it!) Poking is quite rightly regarded as a fault by every shooter and coach of any experience. It is easy to 'poke' at the target without realising it, however, stopping the swing at the vital moment of pulling the trigger.

In contrast, all the accepted techniques of shotgun shooting involve swinging the gun with the target's line of flight, following its imaginary smoke trail. You then pull the muzzles through the target, pulling the trigger when they reach the correct distance in front of the bird. This correct distance varies with the speed of the target, its distance from the gun, and its angle to the gun. Other important factors are the speed of your swing relative to the target, and your reaction time – although your technique should iron out any variations in the latter as much as possible. One day you may be alert and quick to react, in which case the time between your brain giving the order to fire and your finger actually carrying out the operation will be relatively short. The next day, perhaps after a late night, this time may easily be doubled. I try to

23. The author shooting in the snow with his AyA No 2 side-by-side.

minimise the effects of this by slowing my swing as the muzzles reach the desired point ahead of the target, so that, by the time I fire, my reaction speed has little effect – although this is easier said than done. If you swing very quickly through the target, however, it is clear that a small variation in reaction time will mean a miss, since the muzzles will only be in the correct position for a fraction of a second.

Individuals' reaction times are very different, and you should beware of paying too much attention to even a very accurate shot who tells you to fire, for example, a foot in front of the bird. His reaction time is unlikely to be the same as yours, and I have known two shooters to break the same target, one claiming to fire straight at the bird and the other adamant that he gave it a clear yard of lead.

Remember, too, that perfect timing is no use if you vary your technique from one bird to the next, by swinging at a different speed or mounting the gun in a different way for each shot. You should aim to develop a consistent technique, by means of plenty of practice at gun mounting and reading the target.

A good coach will be able to give the less experienced shot a great deal of helpful advice here. He will be able to tell the shooter whether he is missing in front or behind, and from the shooter's description of how much lead he *thinks* he is allowing, will be able to advise the correct sight picture for that particular bird. This is all very well, but there is more to coaching than helping the pupil to hit a given target in a certain set of circumstances. In order to gain the maximum benefit from expert instruction, you should try to understand not only what the coach is telling you, but why – and what he would recommend in a different set of circumstances.

Even with the correct amount of lead, you will not break the target unless you are swinging the gun on the same line as the bird's line of flight. Like giving the correct lead, this is something that comes with practice, and a good coach can be a great help in this, also.

Swinging the gun involves much more than just the arms. The whole body is important, and you must pay attention to foot position, stance and so on, in just the same way as you would if hitting a tennis ball or swinging a golf club. The swing involves the whole body, from the feet upwards. The generally accepted stance is with the left leg (for a right-handed shooter) placed forward, and held relatively straight. Most of the shooter's weight is placed on this leg, and the right is used almost solely for support. Bend forwards slightly at the waist, leaning

53

towards the target as though you were pointing your whole body towards it. A common fault among novices is to lean backwards to counteract the weight of the gun. This makes it virtually impossible to swing smoothly, however, and is not recommended.

In clay pigeon shooting, where you know the direction the target is coming from, and its approximate line of flight, it is possible to position yourself carefully and adopt the correct stance in advance. This is rarely possible in rough shooting, and even on a driven shoot the direction of the birds' flight cannot be predicted accurately. The ideal position is with your left foot pointing in the direction of the place where you intend to kill the target. The shoulders should be at approximately forty-five degrees to this direction. Try to imagine yourself standing on a clock face. Your left foot is placed on the twelve o'clock position, which is in the direction of the target. Your shoulders are at ten o'clock and four o'clock. Now wind your body back to the place where the target will emerge. When you call for the bird, your body will naturally tend to 'unwind' back to the twelve o'clock position, helping you to swing easily and naturally.

Stand with your gun out of your shoulder. This is compulsory for most clay shooting disciplines and, in practice, will be your position when a live bird emerges. The muzzles should be in a direct line between your eye and the target. As your body unwinds, let the muzzles follow just behind the bird, bringing the stock smoothly into your shoulder as you swing. Finally, bring the butt firmly into your shoulder just as the muzzles catch up with the target. Swing through, and fire when you judge the lead to be correct. The action of keeping the muzzles between your eye and the target as you mount the gun encourages you to follow the target's line of flight more accurately, and firing quickly once the butt is in the shoulder reduces the tendency to 'poke'. You should also make a positive effort to follow through, keeping the swing going after you have fired the shot. This, too, makes 'poking' less likely. To give credit where it is due, the basic principles of this technique were developed by the coaches of the Clay Pigeon Shooting Association, who refer to it as 'The Method'.

This technique is all very well for clay shooting, but in rough and game shooting the target's line of flight and point of origin are unpredictable. Therefore it is extremely difficult to begin by making yourself comfortable in the right direction and then wind yourself back towards the bird. More often than not, there is not enough time, and you have to take your shots more hurriedly. However, 'The Method' is excellent training for stance and technique whatever your target, and the same basic principles apply. On the subject of winding the body up for the swing, it is worth noting that, for a right-handed shooter, a right to left swing is more natural than left to right. This means that you have to allow what seems like more lead on a bird crossing left to right.

It is also much easier to swing your body in a straight line from side to side, or a straight vertical line, than it is to follow a diagonal which is a combination of the two directions. By trying to combine the two movements, you are asking your body to co-ordinate two separate movements, which is very difficult to achieve smoothly and confidently. This obviously makes it harder to hit a target which is crossing and rising, for instance. I prefer to adjust my stance so that I am swinging either horizontally or vertically – and not both. With an oncoming, quartering target, for instance, I will turn half sideways and drop the shoulder nearest to the bird, so that my shoulders are parallel to its line of flight. This allows a simple, horizontal swing along the target's 'smoke trail', with no need for any vertical movement.

If I took the same bird by standing square-on, I would have to swing the gun sideways and upwards, and I would tend to make the movements one at a time – first one, then the other, then the first again.

I fear that I may have been a little long-winded in describing style and technique, but even the simplest body movement requires many words to explain. The important thing is to learn how the correct movement actually feels. You can learn a lot more by spending an hour or two with a really good coach than you ever could by reading about it. Quite simply, practice makes perfect.

Balance and handling
Having talked about the technique for shooting a moving target, it is appropriate to look at the features of a gun that contribute to making this easier – or otherwise. The terms balance and handling describe how the gun feels in your hands, and how well it responds to your actions. As such, they are very subjective, and a gun that suits one person's style and technique may be totally unsuitable for another.

This depends largely on your physical characteristics, such as the length of your arms, your strength and build – but also on less measurable factors, personal preference for example. Some people like a long, heavy gun that takes a lot of effort to get swinging, but which continues swinging well. Others will prefer a lighter, more responsive gun.

The type of shooting that you intend to do is an important factor when you consider a gun's balance and handling characteristics. If the targets will be fast and close, as in Skeet or driven partridge shooting, then a light, quick-handling gun is required. If, on the other hand, you plan to shoot Trap, then a heavier gun will be more suitable. Personally, I like a gun which is heavier and longer than average, and I shoot most types of target best with a Trap gun fitted with chokes suitable for the range, quarry and cartridge.

So what are the factors that determine the handling qualities of a gun? One of the most important is the distribution of weight along its length. Most guns are designed to balance around the hinge pin, where

24. It is important to bring the comb of the stock firmly into the cheek, as this left-handed sporting clay shooter is doing here.

the barrels are joined to the action. This places the weapon's centre of gravity nicely between the shooter's hands. But this can be achieved by various means. The weight may be concentrated in the middle of the gun, or more spread out along its length. A gun with a large proportion of its weight between the shooter's hands will feel light and responsive, whereas one with the weight distributed towards the ends will be more sluggish and feel heavier. The scientific way of assessing this is to measure the moment of inertia about the point of balance. Gough Thomas, in his book *Shotguns and Cartridges*, describes a means of suspending it in a cradle on a length of steel wire. The gun is rotated through one hundred and eighty degrees and then released. A stopwatch is used to time exactly one minute, and the number of oscillations that the gun performs in this time gives an idea of its moment of intertia. The smaller the number of swings, the greater is its moment of inertia. This is not an absolute measurement, but it can be used to compare one gun against another, and in this way you can check an unfamiliar gun against one you feel comfortable with.

A gunmaker can alter the balance of a gun by drilling holes into the back of the stock to reduce the weight at the butt end, or inserting lead plugs in the holes to bring the point of balance further back. The holes are covered with a butt plate, or with wooden plugs that match the colour and grain of the wood.

Although alterations such as this are possible, it is not feasible to alter the gun's handling qualities to any substantial degree. It would not be possible to give 'life' to a gun that felt dead in the hands, for example. Far better to choose carefully in the first place than to try to make an unsuitable weapon acceptable by means of major surgery.

7 Gun fitting

In most forms of shotgun shooting you do not hold the gun in the aim for any great length of time; you simply bring it to the shoulder and fire almost immediately. In fact, the quicker you fire once the gun touches your shoulder, the better, at least within reason. Therefore it is vitally important that the gun comes naturally up to the aim, so that it is pointing where you are looking. This is what gun fitting is all about. If the gun does not fit, then it will come up to the shoulder pointing in the wrong direction, and you will have to make an adjustment before firing in order to hit the target. Ideally, the gun should come up to the aim as naturally as pointing your finger; it should feel like an extension of your body.

This ideal is pursued by top gunmakers, who tailor each gun to the individual customer. Cheaper and mass-produced guns are not individually made to fit in this way, of course. Manufacturers making guns by the thousand have to compromise and base the dimensions on the 'average' shooter. This is fine for shooters with the supposedly average measurements, but in practice this applies to only a few people. Consequently most people shoot with a gun that fits less than perfectly.

To complicate matters further, guns may be produced for the average shooter in a particular country. Quite obviously the average Japanese does not have the same measurements as the average Briton.

Gun fitting consists of altering the dimensions of the gun, particularly the stock, so that it suits the individual shooter's physical characteristics. A shooter with a long neck and broad shoulders will need a differently shaped gun from one who is more slightly built.

Modern shooters tend to understand the importance of a well fitting gun more than their predecessors, although the old master gunmakers would tailor their guns to the individual customer. Nevertheless, there are still many shooters today who mistakenly believe that they can shoot equally well with almost any gun. They sometimes argue that, provided you are looking straight down the rib, then there is no reason for missing—in theory at least. There is a lot of truth in this, but the whole idea of gun fitting is to make the gun come up to the shoulder so that the aiming eye is looking down the rib naturally, with no need for last minute adjustments of position. With a rifle, gun fit is less important, since aiming a rifle is a slow, deliberate act. A shotgun, on the other hand, should come up to the correct position without conscious effort – and this can only be achieved consistently with a combination of practice and a well fitting gun.

With a rifle, you look through the rearsight to the foresight, and on to the target, and there is no way in which mounting errors can cause incorrect alignment. With a shotgun, however, there is only the foresight, and the shooter's aiming eye must perform the same function as the rifle's rearsight. Consequently, the position of the aiming eye relative to the barrel is critical. If it is too high, then the shot goes high, and if it is to one side the shot will pass to that side of the target.

The position of the aiming eye is determined by the comb of the stock, assuming that the gun is mounted correctly so that the cheek rests on the comb. The top of the comb should nestle into the hollow of the cheekbone. Altering the shape of the stock will move the eye relative to the barrel, and therefore alter the point of impact of the shot – just as moving the position of a rifle's rearsight would change the position of the group on the target.

Lowering the comb lowers the aiming eye, and so lowers the point of impact. Conversely, a high comb gives a higher point of impact. Most guns are designed so that the gun shoots to the point aim when the eye is looking slightly down on the rib. The normal sight picture includes a small amount of rib, and if you looked exactly along the rib then the shot would go low. This is so that you have a better view of the target when you fire.

The measurement used to define the height of the comb is referred to as the 'drop'. It is measured by placing a straight edge along the rib and gauging the vertical distance from the straight edge to the top of the comb. This should be measured at the point where the shooter's cheek touches the comb when he mounts the gun normally, since this is the point that determines whether the eye looks correctly down the rib.

Comb height can be adjusted by bending the stock vertically up or down at the hand, or by adding or removing material from the comb itself. Lowering the comb can be done quite simply by planing down the wood, followed by re-finishing the wood surface. Raising the comb is less easy to do without making the stock look messy, but it can be done successfully – either with wood chosen to match the stock or with

25. Do-it-yourself gun fitting – a Stevens pump-action with homemade comb raiser and spacer under the butt plate.

a comb raiser of rubber or similar material. I raised the comb of my Stevens pump-action shotgun by simply shaping a piece of softwood and screwing it into position. The result could hardly be described as beautiful, but it improves the gun's fit beyond recognition. Before the alteration, my eye was hidden behind the receiver, but with the comb raiser in place I aim naturally down the rib.

Guns designed to shoot rising targets – as most of them are – are normally made to throw the pattern slightly high of the point of aim. This gives a sort of built in lead for a bird that is rising. Trap guns in particular are designed to shoot high, and it is a feature of Trap weapons that they have high combs.

Comb height should in theory take care of the eye's alignment with the rib in the vertical plane, but there is also the matter of horizontal alignment to consider. In most guns, this is achieved by having the stock bent slightly to one side or the other – to the right for a right-handed shooter. This is known as 'cast-off', or 'cast-on' if the bend is to the left. It allows you to place the butt comfortably in the hollow of your shoulder, and look directly along the rib with your aiming eye. If the gun and its stock were dead straight, then you would look along one side of the barrel, since your eye is not directly above the hollow of your shoulder.

Some mass-produced guns have little or no cast-off, however, which can make life very difficult for the shooter. He will have to tilt his head in order to position it so that he looks straight down the rib. This makes adjustments to the measurements rather complicated, because altering the comb height, for example, will alter the tilt of the head, and require a compensating adjustment to be made to the cast-off.

Alterations to the drop and cast-off of a stock can be done by bending the wood at the hand. This is a tricky operation, which involves heating the wood with hot oil and/or infra-red lamps. The wood becomes pliable when treated in this way, and can be bent and clamped into the required position to set. Great skill is needed to avoid damaging the stock, and this work must be left to an experienced stocker. To make it even worse, many modern guns have a bolt through the hand of the stock, making bending virtually impossible. Even in a traditional side-by-side, the tang of the action, which houses the safety catch, may need to be bent too. If this is necessary, then the metal of the action must be softened and then re-tempered. Once again, this is difficult work, and no job for the amateur.

One unusual and interesting type of stock is the cross-over stock, designed to be mounted in one shoulder while aiming with the opposite eye. This is sometimes prescribed for a shooter who has used a gun normally all his life, and then loses the sight of his master eye. Shooting from the other shoulder would feel unnatural to him, and a cross-over stock enables him to shoot from the same shoulder while aiming with his one good eye. This type of stock is not to be recommended for a beginner who is right-handed and has a left master eye, however. In this case, it is much better to learn to shoot off the left shoulder, or wear a patch over the left eye.

The two basic measurements that I have just described – the cast-off and the drop at comb – are what really determine whether a gun comes up to the aim properly or not. A lot of people attach too much importance to a third measurement, the length of the stock. Although a stock that is much too long or too short for the user will be a handicap, stock length has only an indirect effect on aiming. The reason for this is that changing the length of the stock will cause your cheek to rest on a different part of the comb. Since the comb on most guns slopes downwards from front to back, this will raise or lower your aiming eye relative to the rib. Shortening the stock, for instance, will bring your cheek further up the comb, so raising it and causing you to miss over the top of the target. This is not the case if the gun is fitted with a Monte Carlo type of stock, in which the comb runs parallel to the rib. With such a stock, the cheek can be placed anywhere along the comb's length, and still maintain the correct alignment.

The length of the stock is generally measured from the trigger blade, and this is known as the 'length of pull'. There are three different ways of taking this measurement from the trigger blade: *1.* to the toe of the butt; *2.* to the centre of the butt; and *3.* to the heel. The most important of these three is the length of pull to the centre of the butt. The other two simply tell you the angle of the butt to the line of the barrels – whether it slopes back or forwards, and by how much.

Although the stock length is of limited importance compared to the other two measurements described, it should still fall within certain limits if the shooter is to perform well with it. The stock should not be so long that it catches in your clothing as you bring the gun to your shoulder; and if it is too short, you are likely to break your nose with your hand when you fire and the gun recoils. Between these two extremes is a fairly wide range of measurements that will feel comfortable to you – and that is the important factor. As I have said before, the gun should come up to the shoulder naturally and without conscious effort. You should not have to remember to push it forward as you mount to get the butt past your armpit, and neither should you need to pull it consciously backwards to bed it firmly into your shoulder. Mounting the gun is the only valid test of whether it fits or not. Do not fall into the trap of testing the length by measuring it against your forearm. You will see shooters grasp the hand of the stock with a finger on the trigger, and test whether the butt falls neatly into the crook of the elbow. If it does, they will pronounce the stock length 'right', when in fact it may be anything but.

The stock length is one of the easiest measurements to alter. A section of the wood can be removed and the butt re-finished to shorten the stock, and lengthening pieces or a rubber pad may be used to extend it. As always, it is easier and more satisfactory to remove wood than to add to it, so do not have a stock shortened unless you are sure that it is the right thing to do. Incidentally, I successfully lengthened the stock of my Stevens pump-action by inserting a piece of wood between the end of the stock and the butt-plate. The result was practical, but by no means a craftsman's job and it would have been a disaster on a good quality gun.

The angle of the butt is defined by the length of pull measurements described earlier. Like the length of pull itself, it has little effect on where the gun actually shoots, but it can make a profound difference to how comfortable it is to use. Depending on the shape of your shoulder, you might want the butt to slope forwards or backwards. If the angle is wrong, then the gun's recoil is concentrated on a single point of contact, which will very probably cause bruising. Ideally, the recoil should be transferred across the entire surface of the butt: the whole butt should be in contact with the shoulder. The fit of the butt in the shoulder can be improved by a slight twist so that the toe is angled inwards or outwards, too.

The top gunmakers still build their guns to fit the individual customer. The gunmaker will measure the customer in the same way as a tailor would measure for a new suit. A wide range of measurements is required in order to ensure that the gun fits.

A popular way of measuring a customer is to use a try gun, which is a normal shotgun action and barrels fitted with an adjustable stock. The stock measurements can be altered with a special key, enabling

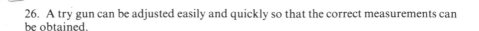

26. A try gun can be adjusted easily and quickly so that the correct measurements can be obtained.

the gun fitter to try out various combinations of measurements in practice. Final adjustments are made after the customer has fired a few shots at a pattern plate. The correct measurements are then noted down and the gun can be produced to the exact specifications required. Some experts prefer not to rely entirely on the try gun, and add an element of experience and judgment rather than taking the try gun's measurements as gospel. The great advantage of the try gun is that it enables ideas and theories to be tested quickly and easily, without the need for expensive and time-consuming adjustment and re-adjustment of the shooter's own gun.

Another frequently used technique consists of looking along the rib from the muzzle end as the shooter holds the gun in the aim – after first making quite sure that the gun is empty, of course. Looking down the rib in this way, it is easy to spot any errors in gun fit or mounting which cause the eye to be out of alignment with the rib.

Gun fitting depends very much on the shooter mounting the gun in the same way time after time. It would be impossible to fit a gun accurately to a shooter who mounted it inconsistently, so it is important to develop a consistent style and keep to it. This is a chicken-and-egg situation, however, because it is easier to mount a well fitted gun accurately and consistently.

8 Chokes, patterns and cartridges

As we have seen in the previous two chapters, placing the pattern on the target – or causing the two to coincide in time and space – depends on many factors, including style and technique, and various aspects of gun fit. But placing the pattern on the target correctly is only part of the story, because there is no guarantee that the shot will be successful even if it is aimed and fired perfectly. If the target is to be broken, or the quarry killed, then the pattern must be effective. In other words, it must contain sufficient pellets close enough together and with sufficient energy, to do the job.

Let us examine the pattern more closely. It consists of a large number of small lead pellets, travelling close together at high speed. If you could stop it in mid-flight, you would find that it spread in all directions – width, height and length. Not all the pellets in the pattern travel in exactly the same direction, nor at the same speed. Because each pellet is subjected to slightly different forces as the shot charge travels up the barrel, and because some pellets are more perfectly formed than others, the pattern becomes more spread out as it moves further from the muzzle.

The standard method used to quantify the pattern thrown by a particular combination of gun and cartridge is to fire at a sheet of paper or a metal pattern plate from a measured distance, normally 40 yards (36.5 metres). The points where the pellets strike the plate show up clearly, particularly if the metal is brushed over in advance with thin whitewash. You can judge the centre of the pattern quite accurately by eye. Then draw a circle of 30 inches (76 centimetres) diameter around this point, and count the number of pellets contained within the circle. This figure is normally expressed as a percentage of the total number of pellets in the original cartridge, and an average is taken over, say, half a dozen shots. Do not forget that this is a two-dimensional measurement that takes no account of the length of the string of shot. This may seem unimportant, since the pellets at the front of the string will strike the plate a few milliseconds before the last, but in certain circumstances it may make a difference. A target crossing the shot string at right angles may pass through only a portion of the pattern, so that the pattern on the plate gives a false impression of the number of pellets likely to hit a target of a given size.

In particular, it is possible to miss the target in front with the front end of the shot string, yet still hit it with the tail end. If you miss behind, however, there is no chance of this – which adds weight to the often-quoted advice to 'miss them in front'.

Various factors influence the spread of the pattern at a given range. The most obvious is choke, but other things such as the type of cartridge and the shape of the chambers are also important.

Choke

Choke is the term that describes the constriction at the muzzle which has the effect of reducing the spread of shot at a given range. The effect is similar to squeezing the nozzle of a hosepipe; the greater the constriction, the narrower the jet of water. In a shotgun, the constriction is very slight – a matter of a few thousandths of an inch. The difference between true cylinder and full choke is just 35 to 40 thousandths of an inch, yet it is sufficient to almost double the number of pellets in the 30-inch circle at 30 yards.

Choosing the ideal degree of choke for a given type of shooting is a tricky business, with several conflicting factors to consider. For instance, a tight choke will give a denser pattern, with a correspondingly greater chance of striking the target with sufficient pellets to score a kill. However, the pattern will also be smaller, requiring greater accuracy to place the pattern on the target in the first place. And if you intend to eat what you shoot, then hitting it with too many pellets is undesirable. A more open choke, on the other hand, may produce a pattern with holes large enough for the target to pass through unscathed. The ideal choke would be a compromise between these two, producing a pattern sufficiently dense to be sure of killing the target, but no more dense than necessary. As a general rule, you should use the least degree of choke that will still give consistent kills with accurately placed shots. If you knew exactly the size and range of the target, then you could calculate precisely the ideal degree of choke. But it is seldom, if at all, that the exact range is known in advance – particularly when shooting live quarry.

So you must choose a compromise that will give good results at the ranges that you expect to shoot, and on the size of target normally encountered. This is relatively easy for clay shooting, particularly the more formal Skeet and Trap. For rough and game shooting, the normally accepted compromise is one quarter choke in the first barrel, and one half or three quarters in the second. This should provide good, clean kills on most quarry species at normal ranges, without 'overkill'. You should learn to exercise restraint, and avoid firing at quarry that is outside normal ranges.

Regulating a gun's chokes is a skilled job, and a gunmaker may take many hours firing at the pattern plate, filing away at the chokes, and re-testing until he is satisfied with the patterns he has achieved. He will look not only for the correct pattern density, but also for uniformity, dividing the circle into segments and counting the number of pellets in each. The care and skill that goes into regulating chokes is yet another of the 'hidden' differences between the top quality gun and a mass-

27. A set of screw-in choke tubes made by Nigel Teague, fitted to the author's Rizzini over-and-under.

produced one. Guns coming off the end of a production line will have chokes measured in thousands of an inch, or hundredths of milli-metres. They will be accurately formed, to within close tolerances – but they will not have been tested and regulated according to the actual patterns they throw. Thus the pattern from a mass produced gun is not likely to be so regular and even as that from a quality, hand-made weapon.

Chamber cones
Another aspect of the gun which influences the pattern is the chamber cones. That is to say, the constriction at the end of the chamber which brings the diameter of the chamber down to that of the barrel. Cham-ber cones may be long, with a shallow angle, or they may be steeply angled and much shorter. In general, a sharp angle will tend to produce a greater spread of shot, largely because it deforms the pellets more than a shallow angle would. Obviously, the more the pellets are de-formed, the more irregularly they will tend to fly through the air, and the more spread out the pattern will be.

I have heard it said that a really expert gunmaker can regulate the patterns almost as effectively by working on the chamber cones as by altering the chokes themselves. The more normal practice is to adjust the chokes themselves, though.

On the subject of choke, it is interesting to note that the important factor is not the actual diameter of the muzzle, but the degree of constriction, and the angle of the walls as they slope in from the bore diameter. If the bore is slightly oversize, then a muzzle diameter slightly larger than the nominal measurement for, say, half choke, would give the same effect as the standard measurement in a bore of normal diameter. One occasionally comes across the so-called recessed choke, in which the barrel is bored out to a greater diameter just before the muzzle, leaving what is in effect a degree of choke in the muzzle – even though it may be the same diameter as the bore. Such chokes are relatively difficult to make, and are not normally seen on shotguns in the field. A variation on this is the retro Skeet choke, which is designed actually to increase the spread of the shot – giving wider patterns than would be achieved with a true cylinder barrel.

The cartridge
It is not only the gun that has an effect on the patterns. The cartridge,

too, has a considerable influence – much more, in fact, than many shooters realise.

The most obvious factor here is the number of pellets in the load. This depends on the weight of shot in the cartridge – $1\frac{1}{16}$ or $1\frac{1}{8}$ ounces in the standard 12 bore load – and the pellets' size. For a given weight of shot, smaller size pellets will give greater pattern density than large ones. This is why patterns are measured in terms of percentages of the total load, rather than a straight number of pellets.

I have already mentioned that deformed shot gives a greater spread of shot than well-rounded pellets. Indeed, in the past, Skeet shooters have loaded square shot and battered shot in an attempt to obtain a greater spread and improve their chances of a kill. Modern clay shooting rules forbid this, however.

Yet the pellets may start their journey up the barrel perfectly round, and become deformed by the forces exerted on them by the wad driving them up the barrel and by the walls of the barrels themselves. Lead shot is hardened during manufacture by the addition of antimony, and manufacturers will add more or less antimony to provide the degree of hardness required. Hard shot is used for long-range loads such as those intended for Trap shooting, while Skeet loads will contain much softer shot which will be more easily deformed and so provide a broader pattern for close-range shooting. Shot pellets may also be coated with a thin layer of another metal – commonly nickel – to improve their performance. Contrary to popular belief, this has virtually no effect on the hardness of the shot, although it does make the pellets considerably smoother. In fact, one of the greatest advantages of nickelled shot is that it flows more freely through the manufacturer's machinery. To the shooter, this means that shot loads may be slightly more uniform from one cartridge to the next.

The velocity of the cartridge also has an effect here. This is an indirect effect: a greater velocity means faster acceleration, which means that the pellets become more deformed. Trap cartridges tend to be some of the fastest, since Trap targets are shot at relatively long ranges, and consequently the shot must be very hard to withstand the force of acceleration without being deformed. The burning characteristics of different powders are used to provide a smooth acceleration in order to minimise this, and to reduce the recoil to an acceptable level.

The wadding in a cartridge provides a cushion for the shot against the force or the burning powder, and more effective wadding will result in less deformation in a given set of circumstances. Alternatively, it may allow a greater velocity for a given level of deformation, depending on what is required.

Manufacturers put a great deal of thought into designing shotgun wads, from the humble, though highly effective, fibre wad to the sophisticated plastic cup wads with compressible pillars and integral sealing skirts. Some plastic wads are combined with a cork or fibre disc to give even greater efficiency. The now familiar cup shaped plastic wad is designed to protect the shot from abrasion as it travels down the barrel. This eliminates another potential cause of deformation, and increases the number of effective pellets in the pattern.

I have avoided talking of pellet deformation as thought it were necessarily a good thing or a bad thing, because it can be either. Depending on the range of the target, you may require an open pattern or a tight one.

So these are the factors influencing the number of pellets in the pattern at a given range, but whether or not they do the job depends also on their energy. This is a function of their mass and velocity (Kinetic energy $= \frac{1}{2}$ [mass $\times$ velocity^2]). A heavy pellet travelling fast obviously has more energy than a light one moving more slowly. A high energy pellet will fly further, and strike the target with more force. Obviously, we want to hit the target with sufficient pellets with enough energy to kill it, but increasing the size and velocity of individual pellets means that there are fewer of them in the pattern, as we have just seen. To an extent, you can increase the power of the cartridge, to fire more shot at faster velocities, but there are severe limitations on this. Let us consider what these are.

First, there is recoil, the 'equal and opposite reaction' to the action of the shot leaving the muzzle. The shooter can only take so much recoil, and, although some people will accept more than others, for most men the standard $1\frac{1}{8}$ ounce load in a 12 bore of normal weight is as much as they can reasonably handle. Where you expect to fire very few shots in a day, and range is an important factor, then you may be prepared to accept heavier loads giving greater recoil, however.

Secondly, there are the technical problems of providing greater power. Manufacturers are constantly looking at new ways of getting more out of a cartridge – making the shot harder, improving the wadding, and using different powders to achieve high velocity with acceptable recoil, for instance. They are restricted in their efforts by the rules for clay pigeon shooting, which specify the bore sizes, weight of shot and so on that may be used in competitions. But it is not just the 'rules of the game' that hold back cartridge performance. As the ammunition is improved and refined, the law of diminishing returns begins to have an effect. For example, as velocity increases, so does air resistance, so that enormous amounts of extra power are required in order to raise the velocity by a significant degree.

The effect of all this is that the shotgun has a maximum practical range of about 45 yards (41 metres) or so, beyond which it is impossible to be reasonably sure of a clean kill. Even with a magnum 12 bore load, you are pushing your luck at much more than five yards further, and it is debatable whether many people can shoot accurately enough to be sure of hitting the mark at that range anyway – on a moving target especially.

In summary, the effectiveness of a given combination of gun and cartridge depends on many factors, some obvious and some less so. For any given situation, you could choose the ideal combination, but the difficulty lies in selecting a combination that is versatile enough to cope with the variety of problems that may be encountered in an unpredictable sport such as rough shooting. This is largely possible in clay shooting, however, particularly in the more formal disciplines such as Skeet and Trap. The shooter's choice of gun and cartridge will be influenced by all this, and also by personal considerations such as the degree of recoil that he finds acceptable.

PART III
PRACTICE

29. A pair of pheasants present a tricky rising shot.

9 Driven game

Driven game shooting is a formal activity, and the movements of the guns, beaters and even the quarry are fairly regimented. Each gun has his allotted place on a given drive, marked by his peg, and he will not normally move from that spot until the drive is over. The beaters go through the selected patch of cover in a straight line, under the instruction of the keeper, and, if all goes according to plan, the birds will rise and fly over the guns in a fairly predictable way.

From the point of view of choosing a gun, driven shooting therefore has its own special requirements. For a start, the shooters are unlikely to walk far carrying their guns, so the weight is less important than it might be. In many cases, the drives will be relatively close together – and if not, then Land-Rovers will be used to transport them from one drive to the next. Although this saves having to carry your gun around, it does pose a great danger to the gun itself. Climbing in and out of a vehicle, along with half a dozen others, and riding along bumpy, rutted tracks, is virtually guaranteed to cause dents and scratches to the wood or metalwork of an unprotected gun. It is advisable to use a canvas gun sleeve, if not a rigid case, in these circumstances.

It is interesting that, even though driven shooters rarely have to walk far with their guns, they tend to choose rather light weapons of perhaps $6\frac{1}{2}$ or 7 pounds (3 or 3.2 kilogrammes). This is all the more surprising when you consider that on a good day one might expect to fire more than one hundred cartridges – which is rather punishing with a light gun. However, game shooters do tend to use less powerful cartridges than their clay shooting counterparts, and this goes some way to explaining why they prefer a lighter weapon.

One reason for choosing a light gun for game shooting is to achieve the better responsiveness and quicker swing that this provides. This is not so important with driven pheasants, but it is essential when shooting low, fast quarry such as driven grouse or partridges. These birds are so speedy, and are often shot at such close ranges, that with a slow, heavy gun one might well never get onto them at all.

Indeed, there has been a swing in recent years towards 25 inch (63.5 centimetres) barrels, rather than the more common 26 inch or 28 inch tubes (66 or 71 centimetres). I have already stated that I prefer longer barrels, and personally I would have great difficulty in shooting even moderately well with 25 inch barrels. Nevertheless, far be it from me to impose my personal preferences on others. The important thing is whether or not a particular feature of a gun suits you. If it does, think long and hard before you allow another to persuade you against it.

But what are the other features of the gun that affect its suitability for driven game shooting? I mentioned earlier in this book that there is a great deal of illogical prejudice against over-and-unders on a formal shoot, and particularly against all kinds of repeaters. This

28. Shooting driven pheasant with a pair of best side-by-sides and a loader. An experienced gun and loader can keep up a phenomenal rate of fire.

leaves only side-by-sides, and if you hope to be invited to shoot regularly, you will be well advised to use one of these guns. I do not think you will be handicapped by restricting yourself to a side-by-side. They are excellent guns, and well adapted to all kinds of game shooting.

On the important subject of bore size, there is really little choice. The 12 bore is the accepted standard not only in this country but all over the world, with the widest range of ammunition available. It is pointless to make life difficult for yourself by choosing, say, a 20 bore – and it denies you the opportunity of borrowing cartridges from a neighbouring shooter if you should run out. The 20 bore is often used as a stepping stone for a beginner, although I doubt its value in this role. I find that the recoil from a 20 bore is actually sharper and more uncomfortable than that of a 12 bore, and there is precious little to choose between the two in terms of weight. The most valid reason for using a 20 bore to my mind is when a youngster would find a standard 12 bore rather large to handle, and might therefore develop a bad style. Even so, there are 12 bores designed for smaller shooters, and at a pinch a standard gun can be altered to fit. I would suggest that the sooner one can move on to the 'real thing', the better.

The next thing to consider is the chokes, and here lies the subject of much debate and disagreement. I would go along with the belief that almost any degree of choke is a bad thing for driven game shooting. The experts will sometimes cite calculations based on a pheasant sized target crossing at 30 yards to back up their case for half choke or even more, but how often at a driven pheasant shoot do you encounter a target this far away, and crossing at ninety degrees?

Far more common is the oncoming, quartering bird, which is shot at little more than 20 yards. All too often I have seen a high proportion of the bag mangled with shot to the point where it is hardly fit for dog meat, while a light charge fired from a cylinder barrel would have brought it down just as surely. It is true that on the best shoots the keeper will endeavour to show high, difficult birds – and in such cases, especially at the back end of the season, there is a strong case for using a little more choke. I do not believe that there is one bird in a hundred that could not be brought down with half choke, however, while too much choke will spoil perhaps half the bag. My own AyA 12 bore side-by-side is bored quarter and half choke, and I often find myself wondering whether this is not too tight for driven shooting. Very rarely do I feel that I would have shot more with tighter chokes.

On the subject of choke, there is one other small moan that I would like to get off my chest. Every gun that I have ever seen has been designed so that the more openly choked barrel is fired first. Even when the gun has a single selective trigger, the normal position of the selector fires the tighter choked barrel second. Yet the one factor common to all forms of driven shooting is that the quarry is coming closer all the time, until it passes overhead. Logically, you want the more tightly choked barrel first, when the target is that much further away. I have tried pulling the rear trigger first on a double triggered gun, but I always find that it is uncomfortable to move my hand forwards for the second shot. No doubt someone has produced a driven game gun with more choke in the first barrel than in the second, but I have yet to come across an example of this.

So far as the gun itself is concerned, there are few other factors that are desirable specifically for driven game shooting. Such things as reliability and speed of reloading are equally valuable in many other situations. I should mention, however, that the barrels of a side-by-side can become very hot through rapid shooting, and may give you painful blisters on the leading hand. The traditional splinter fore-end gives very little protection against this, and some shooters fit a hand guard as an accessory. These hand guards are made of steel covered with black or brown leather, and slip easily over the barrels of a 12 bore side-by-side. I originally fitted one to my AyA because I used it

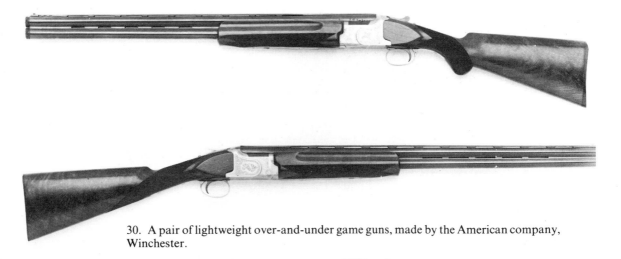

30. A pair of lightweight over-and-under game guns, made by the American company, Winchester.

31. The side-by-side is generally accepted as the most suitable weapon for game shooting. This is a typical driven pheasant – approaching the shooter from directly in front.

for clay shooting, but I have been glad of it on occasions when game shooting, too.

Rapid reloading is not required as often as one might think on the driven shoot, but it is infuriating to miss opportunities when one may have only one good stand in the day's shooting. The side-by-side is probably the fastest shotgun to reload and fire repeatedly, and various

32. A covey of partridges over the line. These fast, low-flying birds require a gun that fits well and swings easily.

adaptations have been developed over the years to make rapid shooting easier. One that has persisted in some of the best guns to the present day is the so-called self-opening action, which flies open under spring pressure when you push the top lever across. With one hand you can open the gun and eject the fired shells, while the other hand reaches for the next pair of cartridges. Whether or not you are shooting with a loader, this can make the whole process much easier and quicker.

So much for the gun, but what are the cartridges most suited to driven game shooting? The most commonly used, and to my mind the most appropriate, are the paper cased, fibre wadded shells loaded with $1\frac{1}{16}$ of size 6 shot – such as Eley's Grand Prix. In certain circumstances, there is a good case for using an even lighter load such as the 1 ounce, which has in fact enjoyed quite a revival in recent years.

Let us examine why these loads have become so widely accepted among game shooters. First, the paper case and fibre wads will rot away to almost nothing in a few months. If plastic cases are used, then the pegs where the guns stand soon become littered with the empty shells, which will still be there the following year unless the keeper takes the trouble to pick them up. Although research has shown that plastic cases have no ill effects when fed to livestock, they are certainly very unsightly, and some farmers are reluctant to believe that they are really completely harmless. The same applies to the plastic wads, which can be seen on some shooting grounds covering the area in front of the stands like a layer of dirty snow.

The quantity of shot in a cartridge for driven shooting must obviously be sufficient to make a clean job of killing the quarry, but it should not be so heavy that the recoil is uncomfortable or tiring after

33. Two beaters carrying the bag from one drive at a Sussex pheasant shoot.

a day's shooting. The $1\frac{1}{16}$ ounce load has been chosen to meet these requirements in the relatively light traditional game gun, and it performs extremely well. It will kill cleanly at normal ranges, yet most shooters find its recoil quite comfortable. The lighter 1 ounce load is chosen by those who suffer from gun headache, or simply find it more comfortable and do not expect to encounter very high birds. I decided to try 1 ounce loads at a North Yorkshire driven pheasant shoot recently, and was pleasantly surprised to find how effective they were, and how light on the shoulder – even after two days of splendid shooting. As a result of this experience, I would be quite confident to use these light loads at all but the tallest of high pheasants. As always, the most important factor is whether or not you aim the shot correctly; degrees of choke and weight of shot come a poor second in my list of priorities.

Finally, the shot size. Number 6 has long been regarded as the ideal for all types of live quarry shooting, with the exception of very large birds such as capercaillie or small species like snipe. Size 6 shot gives a good pattern with the normal combination of choke and range, and the individual pellets retain just sufficient striking energy out to maximum shotgun ranges. If you study the table of optimum shot sizes in that mine of useful information, the *Eley Shooter's Diary*, you will see that size 6 shot is among those recommended for almost all the quarry listed. Certainly, my own experience of shooting live quarry has almost all been with size 6 shot, and I have never had any reason to doubt its effectiveness.

10 Rough shooting

The term rough shooting covers a multitude of different activities, from ferreting to pigeon shooting, from vermin control to walking-up grouse. It is a collective term for almost any kind of live quarry shooting in which the shooter goes in search of the quarry himself, perhaps aided by a dog or ferret, rather than have the game driven over him by beaters. Rough shooting is therefore almost infinitely variable and, for me at least, there lies its charm. I have spent many, many hours rough shooting, and each one of them has been different and special in its own way.

34. Ferreting tends to provide short-range snap shooting – requiring a light gun firing a relatively small charge of shot.

83

All this has a considerable bearing on the choice of the best combination of gun and cartridge for the sport. The quarry may be shot at very close range, for example when ferreting; it may be at very long range, such as a pigeon flighting high overhead; or it may be somewhere in between, perhaps a duck coming into a small flight pond. Furthermore, the quarry may be going straight away, directly towards you, or crossing at any angle.

Naturally there is no single combination of gun and cartridge that will be ideal for all these very different situations. Indeed, it can be hard to choose one that will even cope adequately with them all. But there is no need to cover every eventuality with a single combination. You are never going to tackle every type of rough shooting in a single day, so why not vary your equipment to suit the circumstances? This

35. These two rough shooters are using side-by-sides, but other types of shotgun are equally suitable.

does not necessarily mean spending a great deal of money on several different guns, because you can vary the performance of a single gun by a surprising amount, simply by changing cartridges to match the target. In fact, there is a strong argument for using the same gun for all your shooting. This way you will become all the more familiar with its feel and handling, and you are more likely to develop a good, consistent style. I prefer to do this when I can, and change the cartridge as I feel necessary. It is astounding how much this can alter the gun's performance. An interesting exercise is to use one gun, and the same barrel, to fire a series of different cartridges at a pattern plate or sheets of paper. Even though they are fired through the same barrel, with the same degree of choke, you will find that the results are often poles apart. Some cartridges, perhaps those with plastic cup wads, will produce tighter patterns, while others are much more widely spread. The results are difficult to predict, since no two barrels give identical results, even with shells from the same box. However, a few minutes carrying out your own experiments will soon tell you what to expect from your own gun.

Normally, fibre wads will give less tight patterns than plastic wads, and you can alter the effective choke by quite a considerable amount in this way. If you try different clay shooting cartridges, as well as game shells, you will find the patterns vary even more. Trap shells produce tight patterns, while those designed for Skeet spread more across the pattern plate. However these cartridges are normally available only in clay shooting shot sizes – 7, 8 and 9 – none of which is suitable for most game species.

Rough shooters are not restricted by a set of rules to particular weights of shot in the same way as clay shooters, however, so you can also choose from the wide range of different loads available. These are from $\frac{15}{16}$ ounce in the little one-inch 12 bore shells, right up to magnum loads of $1\frac{3}{4}$ or even 2 ounces. I will normally try to select my cartridges according to the expected range and size of quarry, so, for ferreting rabbits, which normally involves very short ranges, I would use a one-inch cartridge – or at most a 1 ounce load. For medium range, and what might be called 'general' rough shooting, I normally use a standard $1\frac{1}{16}$ ounce game load, and for long range a heavier weight of shot – perhaps even a magnum load of $1\frac{3}{4}$ ounces, always provided that the gun is proofed to the necessary pressure.

I prefer not to vary the shot size too much, keeping to number 6 in

36. A folding single barrel shotgun, the Lincoln. This is a cheap but reliable weapon which might be used for rough shooting.

all but the most exceptional cases – although I might use 7's for small quarry like snipe, and 5's for ducks at long range. Larger quarry such as geese and foxes are another matter altogether, and I would choose size 1 or even larger for these species.

Let us turn now to the aspects of the gun itself that make it more or less suitable for rough shooting. The basic requirements are familiar – that it should be well fitted to the shooter, reliable, and in good order. It is best to choose a 12 bore, since this allows a much wider variety of ammunition than the other bore sizes.

It is possible that you may use different guns for different forms of rough shooting – perhaps a light, fast handling gun for ferreting and walked-up game birds, and a heavier, longer barrelled weapon for pigeon shooting, for example. I always use my AyA side-by-side for rabbit shooting, for instance, whereas I select the heavier, slower handling over-and-under for longer-range targets.

However, I said earlier that it is desirable for various reasons to use the same gun for all your shooting. If you do this, it should be as versatile as possible. Unfortunately, a feature that is excellent for one type of shooting may be a positive disadvantage for another, and any multi-purpose weapon is bound to be a compromise. You will un-doubtedly choose the length of barrel that you feel most comfortable with for the 'average' kind of shot. However, this will be rather too long and unresponsive for the closest targets, and will lack sufficient inertia for the longest. Even so, it will probably be perfectly adequate for ninety per cent of your shooting – and many people would feel that it is better to use a familiar gun all the time rather than chop and change.

Similarly, you may choose a gun proofed for magnum cartridges to

37. OPPOSITE. ABOVE: Shooting walked-up grouse in the Scottish Highlands. The gun, which is not visible in the photograph, was a side-by-side.

38. BELOW: The author's AyA No 2 side-by-side shotgun, which is used for all types of game and clay shooting.

39. The rough shooter's gun will have to withstand fairly extreme weather conditions.

give you a wider choice of loads. Unfortunately, magnum guns are generally heavier and longer in the barrel than those designed only for standard shells, and this too may be a drawback in certain circumstances.

The same could be said of the normal types of choke, in which the constriction is a part of the bore and therefore cannot be altered – at least not without irreversibly boring the choke out to a wider diameter. You are lumbered with whatever choke your gun has, even though you may want true cylinder for close shooting and three quarter or full choke for distant targets. But there are a number of variable choke devices that will enable you to swap chokes at a moment's notice, so you can adapt the one gun for different types of shooting.

These devices generally work on one of two principles. First, there is the type that has a screw collar. Screwing down the collar compresses a set of leaves that form the muzzle, so constricting them and effectively tightening the choke in the barrel. The second type has separate screw-in tubes, which are removed and replaced by means of a special key. Personally, I prefer this type to the screw collar type, mainly because I believe that a tube must give a better pattern. After all, the muzzle has to be split into segments, with gaps between, in order to form the screw-collar type. Another advantage of screw-in tubes is that they do not enlarge the muzzle beyond its normal diameter. The screw-collar type, on the other hand, creates quite a bulge at the end of the barrel, which I find distracting.

I have already mentioned that I had my Rizzini over-and-under fitted with screw-in choke tubes, and this increased its versatility enormously. Not only that, but my interest in choke was heightened, and I found myself thinking long and hard about the correct choke for each shot – probably thinking too much, in fact. I am now quite happy to use the gun for almost every kind of shooting open to me, and I feel very confident with it.

These screw-in choke tubes can be fitted to almost any gun, provided it has sufficient thickness in the muzzle walls. The work requires the gun to be proofed again, but this should not be a problem and only takes a day or two extra. Even double barrelled shotguns can have screw-in choke tubes fitted, which is a problem with the screw collar type. Quite a few modern guns – both side-by-sides and over-and-unders – can be bought with screw-in chokes fitted, and an example is the Winchester Winchoke. I would suggest that a gun of this type is

89

the closest that you can ever get to a truly 'all-round' weapon.

My personal choice of gun for rough shooting would be a side-by-side or over-and-under, fitted to perfection, and with barrels that were a little on the long side rather than short. It would be fitted with screw-in choke tubes or, if not, with quarter and half choke. It would have two triggers, so that I could easily select the choke required for each target as it appeared. Finally, it would not be an expensive gun. There is little point in taking out a gun that cost so much money that you are terrified of scratching it every time you climb a fence or push through a patch of cover. I am not careless with my guns when I am rough shooting, but sooner or later it is going to be scratched, and it would be an awful shame if it was a top quality gun.

So that is my 'ideal' rough shooting gun. Other people will have their own ideas, because one's choice of gun, particularly for this form of sport, is a very personal thing. When you have carried a gun over all kinds of terrain, and used it to bag many different types of quarry, it becomes much more than a weapon, and almost an old friend. Simply holding it will bring back memories of happy days in the field or on the hill – and that is the real test of a rough shooting gun.

11 Wildfowling

Traditionally, the wildfowler has used some of the largest, biggest bored guns available in an attempt to gain a few extra yards of effective range. Wildfowling is practised on large expanses of marsh, where the duck are very wary and often fly over at extreme range. Since chances are few and far between, it is understandable that the shooter should want to maximise his chances by firing a heavy load of shot, often through a tightly choked barrel. Over the years, many gunmakers have produced special wildfowling guns. These are usually characterised by their long barrels, heavy weight, tight choke and utilitarian appear-

40. Wildfowling with a standard 12 bore side-by-side game gun.

ance. Even the better grades of wildfowling gun generally show little embellishment, and often have features designed to confer extra strength, such as a metal butt-plate. This is important on the marsh, since a wildfowler's gun will be subjected to extremely harsh conditions – and will probably not receive the cossetting that most game guns enjoy.

A wildfowler may throw his gun into the bottom of a boat, along with a haversack of gear and a string of decoys. When he reaches his chosen position, he will flounder about in the mud, probably dunking his gun it it. In a short time, his hands will be covered with mud and soaked with salt water, and this is immediately transferred to the gun. At the end of the day, the gun goes in the back of the car, together with all the dirty gear and a soggy labrador – and, if he has been lucky, a few salty duck. Even assuming that our imaginary wildfowler cleans the gun carefully when he gets home, removing the salt and dirt and wiping it over with oil, a day's wildfowling is still quite an ordeal for any weapon. No wonder that wildfowling guns are made strong and sturdy. Even if they survive the attacks of salt and water, the mud and dirt that are an inevitable part of wildfowling could easily cause a jam in the mechanism of a delicate weapon. Some people manage to keep their guns cleaner than others, of course. If I spend a day on the marsh with my father, for instance, his gun will still look quite clean at the end of the day, while mine is scarcely distinguishable from a piece of muddy driftwood, and grates horribly as I open and close it.

It is obvious that a wildfowling gun must therefore be able to accept rough treatment, and must not be prone to jamming. To my mind, this makes repeaters, and particularly automatics, somewhat unsuitable for wildfowling, although I have seen many wildfowlers use them very successfully. Perhaps they are better at keeping their guns clean than I. Certainly, if I took an automatic onto the marsh, it would be blocked with mud and completely unserviceable within half an hour. This need for ruggedness and reliability also explains why some of the more unusual mechanisms – such as the Martini-Henry and the bolt-action – are sometimes used by wildfowlers. They are among the strongest actions ever made, and as such have a clear advantage for wildfowling.

However, the familiar break-barrel action is probably used by more wildfowlers than any other, and this would not be the case were this mechanism not up to the job. In fact, the side-by-side is possibly the most widely used for wildfowling, and this is entirely due to practical

41. In a situation like this, it is all too easy for pieces of weed or mud to block the shotgun's mechanism.

reasons, and not the illogical prejudice that exists on the formal game shoot. Wildfowlers tend to be loners, both in the way that they pursue their sport and in temperament, and they would pay little attention to the disdainful looks of other sportsmen – even if there was anyone else around to notice what gun they were using.

In just the same way, no-one need feel embarrassed about using heavier than normal cartridges for wildfowling. It is quite usual to shoot duck with magnum cartridges loaded with perhaps $1\frac{3}{4}$ ounces

42. It is impossible to avoid getting salt water and mud onto the gun when wildfowling in conditions like this.

(49.5 grammes) of shot – and to shoot geese with a normal game load would be positively cruel. A goose is a big, heavy bird that takes a lot of stopping, and there is no excuse for using a less than adequate load. This need for heavy cartridges explains why wildfowlers use heavy guns, despite the fact that they will probably have to carry the weapon across several miles of very difficult terrain. A heavy load requires a heavy gun if the recoil is not to be ridiculously harsh.

There was a time when the majority of wildfowlers would use large bore guns – perhaps 10 bore, 8 bore or even 4 bore – in order to fire these heavy weights of shot. But today's weapons, and cartridges also, have been improved to the point where a magnum proofed 12 bore can fire a sufficient weight of shot for most purposes. Since the 12 bore has been adopted all over the world as the standard gauge, it is wise to follow suit, unless you plan to load your own cartridges. It is virtually impossible to buy commercially manufactured shells in anything larger than 12 bore today. Perhaps you might find a specialist shop selling 10 or even 8 bore cartridges, but I would be most surprised to hear of anyone making quantities of 4 bore shells. Some enthusiasts use the 8 bore diesel engine starter cartridges – as used to start railway engines, for instance – as a basis for their own 8 bore loads. For the larger bores, the standard practice is to make up your own cartridge cases by winding cartridge paper round a piece of wooden dowel. In contrast to this, almost any high street gunshop up and down the country will stock magnum 12 bore cartridges in a variety of shot sizes. In those areas where wildfowling is popular, you will find a good selection of suitable 12 bore cartridges in stock.

Another important factor to the wildfowler is that his gun must be easy to operate in difficult conditions, and with cold, numb and often gloved hands. Wildfowling guns often have coarser chequering, cut deeper and with fewer lines to the inch, than you would find on a game gun. This provides a surer grip in difficult conditions. Similarly, pistol grip stocks and beavertail fore-ends are common for the same reason. Another feature of wildfowling guns is that they often have prominent ribs, with a coarsely cut chequered or ribbed pattern, to give a good sight line in poor light.

One advantage of a repeater on the marsh is that the cartridges are kept safe and relatively dry in the magazine tube. When you have fired, there is no need to fumble for a fresh shell, and possibly drop it in the mud as you try to insert it in the breech. Instead, a new cartridge is

loaded into the magazine tube once the quarry has gone. Against this, there is the argument that you are unlikely to have a chance to fire more than a couple of shots at a time, normally with a gap of perhaps a couple of hours before another opportunity presents itself. In these circumstances, a repeater offers no advantage over a break-barrel gun, and has the disadvantage of being more liable to jam in adverse conditions.

Although traditionally wildfowlers use magnum loads in heavier than average, specially designed guns, there is also a good case for using a perfectly standard game gun on the marsh, especially if you do a lot of shooting with such a weapon. The reasoning is simple enough, and contains plenty of good sense. If you are familiar with the handling and general feel of a particular gun, which you use regularly, then it is disruptive to change to a completely different weapon for wildfowling. Instead of the normal fast, easy handling, you find yourself struggling with a slow, heavy brute of a gun, and your normal timing and technique goes to pieces. Instead of your regular shooting experience standing you in good stead, it is actually counting against you.

In the same way, a tight choke is a handicap on a medium range bird because it requires more accuracy to hit the target. Certainly, it may provide a kill on a long shot that might otherwise have escaped, but you should ask yourself how much of your wildfowling quarry will actually be at extreme range. I know the confidence that comes with firing a heavy load of shot through a tight choke; but I also know the feeling when that confidence is shattered by a succession of misses at targets that really do not warrant anything more than $1\frac{1}{16}$ ounces (32 grammes) of shot and half choke.

I have not acquired a vast amount of wildfowling experience, but I have spent enough time on the marsh to know that not all the shots are at extreme range, by a long chalk. In fact, I know of one very experienced wildfowler who uses a 20 bore with standard game cartridges for virtually all his fowling – and he regularly brings home more than his fair share of the day's bag. Personally, I like to use a heavier than normal cartridge, but I would not feel unduly handicapped if I was forced to use a normal game gun and cartridge combination.

43. OPPOSITE, ABOVE: Three wigeon cross the wildfowler's hide, in range of his magnum 12 bore, but a long shot for a standard game weapon.

44. BELOW: A magnum 12 bore in use – a popular choice for wildfowling.

Selecting your shots carefully, and knowing when not to pull the trigger, is an important part of shooting, and a very powerful gun can tempt you into firing at quarry that is out of range, simply by boosting your confidence too much. If you use a gun and cartridge that are closer to your familiar combination, then you are better able to make an accurate judgment of whether or not a target is in range.

When I go wildfowling, I normally use one of my break-barrel rough or game shooting guns, but with a more powerful cartridge. Care is

45. A young wildfowler using an over-and-under 12 bore shotgun – an unusual choice for this type of shooting.

needed to avoid choosing a cartridge that is unsuitable for the gun, however. The majority of 12 bore guns will take a $2\frac{3}{4}$ inch (70 milli-metre) cartridge. (The measurement refers to the length of the chamber and the fired cartridge case, not the closed, unfired cartridge, inciden-tally.) A standard 12 bore is often proofed for a maximum service pressure of $3\frac{1}{4}$ tons per square inch, which allows a cartridge more powerful than a normal game load. I would not recommend that a gun should be used with the largest possible load on a regular basis,

46. Wildfowling guns are exposed to very harsh conditions. The canvas sleeve is a wise precaution.

however, as this could strain the mechanism. In any case, the recoil is likely to be more than you can comfortably handle. For a magnum load, the gun must be proofed to a higher pressure, and for the sake of comfort, it should be rather heavier than a standard weapon. In addition, some magnum cartridges require a 3 inch (76 millimetres) chamber rather than the standard $2\frac{3}{4}$ inches (70 millimetres). If in any doubt, you should consult a gunsmith, who will examine the proof marks on the gun as well as the condition of the barrels and action. Even if the proof marks indicate that the gun should be able to withstand a powerful cartridge, corrosion or damage could have rendered it unsafe. Pitting on the barrel walls, dents, or wear on the locking mechanism, for instance, could all make it unsafe.

To summarise my comments on shotguns for wildfowling, by all means use a more powerful combination of gun and cartridge, provided it is safe and you are able to shoot well with it. But do not let yourself be fooled into thinking that it will somehow magically bring down birds that are very high and fast. By choosing a tightly choked, long range weapon, you are actually making things harder for yourself, not easier.

12 Clay pigeon shooting

In clay pigeon shooting, as in the competitive forms of any sport, one's equipment as well as skill is tested to the limit. Skill and aptitude should normally be the deciding factors, but it is fair to say that having the right equipment is a considerable advantage – and, conversely, you would be handicapped by using a gun and cartridge that were less than ideal for the job in hand. I have already mentioned that clay shooters place great emphasis on selecting their equipment, and are perhaps too ready to chop and change in the hope of finding a magic combination that will take them to the top.

This attitude, combined with the particular requirements of the different clay disciplines, has meant that highly specialised shotguns have been developed not just for the simple divisions of Sporting, Skeet and Trap shooting, but even for the sub-divisions of these disciplines. Hence we find guns intended solely for shooting Down-the-Line, or for Olympic Trap, for example. For the purposes of this chapter, I will deal with the three basic disciplines separately, mentioning the sub-divisions as appropriate.

Sporting
Sporting clay shooting is the discipline that is most like rough shooting – and, incidentally, my favourite form of clay shooting. At a Sporting shoot you will encounter targets flying directly away from you, straight towards you, and everything in-between – all at varying heights and speeds, and shot in a 'natural' setting. Each stand is named after a particular type of quarry that it is supposed to represent and imitate – so you may have driven grouse targets, springing teal, woodcock, pigeon and many more. In fact, the skill of the course designer lies in making the targets as varied and as interesting as possible. In theory at least, no two Sporting shoots should ever be the same, and each one has the mark of its designer stamped upon it in a very personal way.

Now, what does this mean in terms of choosing your gun and cartridges? Quite obviously, one of the principal requirements is for versatility. If the targets may vary so widely, then you must choose a gun, or guns, that will cope with the whole range of possibilities. This brings me back to my comments on guns for rough shooting. The gun should fit you well, and swing easily on medium range birds, so that it is neither too sluggish for fast, close work nor too light and wavering for long range targets. Similarly, you can choose different cartridges to make the best use of the chokes available to you – and ideally the gun will have screw-in choke tubes which you can alter to suit the target.

Note that I mentioned the possibility of using more than one gun. This is permitted in Sporting clay shooting under English rules, and many shooters take advantage of this by using a Trap gun for the longer targets and a Skeet gun for the close range birds. However, in the International version, shot under FITASC rules, only one gun is permitted. Your gun is marked with an official sticker when you enter, and even a change of barrel or choke tube is not allowed. The reason for this is that FITASC Sporting is supposed to represent rough shooting as closely as possible, and in the real thing there is little opportunity to change guns or barrels. Even if there was time, few people would want to carry the extra weight with them around the shoot. Whether or not you agree with this argument, the rules are rigidly enforced, so the International Sporting shot is lumbered with his two barrels – or one if he uses an automatic – with which to tackle everything that the course may have in store. The only adjustment he can make is to select different cartridges to suit the various targets. A serious FITASC Sporting shooter will pattern his gun with many different cartridges, so he has a clear idea of how each will perform, and his choice of cartridge for a particular bird will be based on solid fact rather than mere guesswork. FITASC Sporting rules allow a wider choice of cartridges than do those for English Sporting, since you may use $1\frac{1}{4}$ ounce (35.4 grammes) of shot in the International discipline. This may sound a lot, but it is certainly necessary on some FITASC targets, which may consist of a tiny 'mini' clay target at extreme range.

As with all clay shooting, the over-and-under is the most popular type of gun for Sporting, although other types may sometimes be seen. The side-by-side is very rarely used, except at small club events and special classes for side-by-sides at bigger competitions. There is a class for side-by-sides at the annual British Open Sporting Championship of Great Britain, for example.

The over-and-under is well suited to clay shooting, since it offers a precise, uncluttered sight line and little muzzle flip. Additionally, there is a terrific choice of different fittings and specifications for over-and-unders, which is not matched by the choice in other forms of shotgun. I would not hesitate to recommend an over-and-under as the most obvious and sensible choice for clay pigeon shooting.

However, there are always one or two shooters who are the exception to the rule. Duncan Lawton, for example, one of the world's top Sporting shots, always uses a Remington automatic. He has told me that this began when he learned to shoot with an automatic – and ever since then he has found no reason to change. In particular, he dislikes the harsher recoil of break-barrel guns. However, I suspect that even he would use an over-and-under had he learned to shoot with a different weapon – and would perform just as well as he does now with his rather unusual choice.

47. The over-and-under is used by the vast majority of clay pigeon shooters in the UK.

48. Duncan Lawton, the Sporting clay shot, competing with his Remington semi-automatic.

Skeet

Skeet shooting, like Sporting, falls into two main categories – English and International Skeet. The basic layout is very similar for each, although the targets in International, or ISU, Skeet, fly considerably faster, and there is an unpredictable delay of up to four seconds after you call for the bird. The International discipline therefore calls for faster reactions, a faster swing, and snappier shooting altogether.

The basic Skeet layout consists of two trap houses: a 'low' house on the right and a 'high' house on the left. The shooting positions are arranged in a semi-circle between the two houses, and the targets are set to cross half way between the two houses, angled slightly outwards from the shooter. A round of Skeet involves shooting pairs of birds – one from each house – from each of the different positions, providing a selection of crossing targets at various angles and ranges. The important features to remember in choosing a Skeet gun are that the targets are fast, requiring a quick swing, and are always shot at relatively close range. This means that for Skeet you require a short-barrelled, fast handling gun which comes up quickly and precisely to the aim. A broad rib is also an advantage, since it leads the eye well towards the target without hesitation. Clearly, the gun must fit well so that you can bring it swiftly into your shoulder without the need to correct your aim once the gun is in position.

The choke for a Skeet gun need never be any tighter than true cylinder. This amount of choke – or, in fact, no choke at all – combined with $1\frac{1}{8}$ ounces (31.9 grammes) of size 9 shot, gives a pattern that is dense enough to break any Skeet target at the ranges involved. Using a tighter choke will simply make it harder to hit the target. In fact, various methods have been tried to widen the spread of shot for Skeet shooting, in an attempt to make more effective use of the pellets available. Some Skeet guns have counter-bored chokes known as retro-chokes, for instance. Skeet cartridges, too, are designed to spread the charge of tiny pellets as widely as possible. If the rules did not forbid it, I expect that many shooters would use shot consisting of square or polygonal pellets, which would also widen the pattern.

Another common feature of Skeet guns is slots cut in the muzzle to deflect some of the escaping gases sideways and upwards. This has the

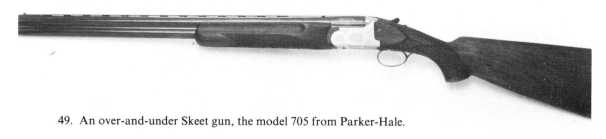

49. An over-and-under Skeet gun, the model 705 from Parker-Hale.

effect of reducing muzzle flip still further than you would normally find in an over-and-under – and so makes it easier to take a well aimed second shot without delay.

Skeet guns generally have 26 inch (66 centimetre) barrels, and the weight of the gun is distributed towards the middle and rear of the gun to promote fast handling. Although this is fine in theory, some shooters find that it makes the gun difficult to swing smoothly. To counteract this, you can attach small weights to the muzzle end of the barrels – and certain makes of Skeet gun are supplied with weights that can be bolted onto the side ribs at the muzzle end for this reason. Personally, I am not a fan of very short barrels and light muzzles, and if I shot Skeet regularly I would certainly want to alter the balance of most Skeet guns in this way.

Trap

Of the three basic disciplines, Trap divides into the greatest number of different categories. Under the one umbrella term, there are Down-the-Line, Automatic Ball Trap, FITASC 5-Trap Universal Trench, and Olympic Trap. Additionally, in some Mediterranean countries such as Italy, it is still possible to shoot live pigeons released from cages in front of the shooter. This was the origin of Trap shooting in this country but was long since banned, quite rightly in my opinion, by animal welfare laws.

The many Trap disciplines are all very different in the speed of the targets, the angles at which the birds are shot, and the distance between Trap and shooter. They also require different degrees of skill – and some would say, different kinds of skill – and it is rare to find a shooter who excels at more than one or, at most, two of them. However, they have certain basic similarities which allow broad generalisations about the type of gun that is most suitable.

All Trap targets are thrown from a position in front of the shooter, so that they fly away from him – rising slightly and usually at an angle so that they are not flying directly away in a straight line. The angle is varied at random, and the shooter cannot predict exactly where the target will go. An important point to note is that the clay pigeon is presented edge-on to the shooter, so the area that he must hit is very small. Also, in Trap shooting you can call for the bird with the gun already mounted in your shoulder – so it does not need to be mounted quickly. You can position the gun correctly in advance, ensuring that your eye is looking properly down the rib and that the butt is nestling well into your shoulder. Only when you are satisfied that all is as it should be do you call for the target.

Although the exact angle of the bird is unpredictable, Trap shooting does not call for the speed of swing that is necessary in, say, Skeet shooting. Instead, you need a smooth, steady movement and a more precise aim, as opposed to an instinctive 'swipe' at a fast moving target. It is generally agreed that this comes with long, heavy barrels – perhaps 28 inches (71 centimetres), 30 inches (76.2 centimetres) or even longer. The rib of a Trap gun is normally fairly thin, to give a more precise aim, and is raised to give a better view of the target. Furthermore, a Trap gun's rib will be ramped at the breech end, effectively tilting the barrels slightly upwards so that the gun shoots high of the point of aim. This provides a certain amount of built-in lead above the target, reducing the forward allowance needed to compensate for its rising

50 In Down-the-Line clay shooting, the target is seen sideways-on, offering a relatively small area – hence the need for a fairly tight choke.

trajectory. For the same reason, the stock of a Trap gun has a high comb, so that the aiming eye tends to look down upon the rib. One common type of Trap stock is the Monte Carlo, which has a section of comb that runs parallel to the barrels. You can place your cheek anywhere along this type of comb without altering the relative alignment of eye and rib.

Finally, the ideal degree of choke for Trap shooting is the subject of much discussion and disagreement. There is a school of thought that nothing short of full choke will do for these small, distant targets. However, I feel that this is rather extreme, and many experienced Trap shooters seem to agree with this point of view. One could work out the theoretically ideal degree of choke by patterning the gun/cartridge combination at the appropriate range, and then checking the resulting

52. Although the over-and-under is most commonly used for clay pigeon shooting, some people prefer other types of gun – as shown by the range of weapons seen in this photograph.

51. OPPOSITE: Trap shooting with an over-and-under. The cup-shaped objects on stands are part of the acoustic target release system.

109

patterns for holes large enough for a clay target to slip through edge-ways. Once the pattern contained a hole of this size, you could say that the choke was not tight enough. As with all pattern experiments, however, this would apply only to the gun and cartridge combination under test, so this is an exercise that the individual shooter would have to carry out for himself. The results would not necessarily apply to another gun and cartridge combination. I would expect that, with the excellent modern cartridges now available, half or three-quarter choke would be sufficient for the first shot, and full choke might be tighter than necessary even for the second.

As always, however, one of the most important factors is the confidence that the shooter has in his equipment. I have seen people perform wonders with guns that the experts would have deemed totally unsuitable, simply because they themselves did not doubt that it could do the job. And, conversely, the finest equipment available is wasted if you spend your time worrying that it may not be adequate.

The law

Firearms legislation is a thorny subject. The police have a habit of releasing statistics on armed crime at regular intervals, often with the implied assumption that, if firearms of all types were controlled more strictly, the figures would make less disturbing reading. Personally, I doubt that this is true. After all, the criminal does not take the trouble to apply for a shotgun or firearm certificate, and he does not buy his arms legitimately from a high street gunshop. Tighter controls would not necessarily have any effect at all on the incidence of armed crime, but would most certainly make it even more troublesome for the bona fide sportsman to pursue his hobby.

Regardless of your views on the subject, it is the duty of every sportsman to respect and abide by the law. By stepping outside it, he brings discredit upon all shooters – and increases the likelihood of more restrictive legislation.

The law relating to shotguns is rather simpler and less restricting than that on weapons that the law classes as firearms. Quite simply, to own or buy a shotgun, you must possess a Shotgun Certificate. You apply for this through your local police station, and the form must be endorsed by a doctor, J.P., bank manager, or 'person of similar standing'. The only circumstances in which you do not require a Shotgun Certificate are when you borrow a shotgun from the owner of private land and use it in his presence on his land. There are very few reasons why the police may refuse to grant you a Shotgun Certificate. Certain classes of convicted criminal may not hold one, for instance. If you have problems in obtaining a Shotgun Certificate, or you find that the police try to impose restrictions on when and where you can shoot, then contact the British Association for Shooting and Conservation. They will assist their members in such cases – and if you are not already a member of the BASC, then you should be. Their address may be found in Appendix III.

There are also restrictions on young people and their use of shotguns. If you are under fifteen, you may be given a shotgun as a gift (provided you have a Shotgun Certificate, of course) but you may only use it if you are supervised by a person over twenty-one. There are very few exceptions to these general rules, and it is wise to check the relevant Home Office publications.

You will also need a Game Licence, which can be obtained from a Post Office, if you intend to shoot species defined as game. These are: pheasant, partridge, grouse, ptarmigan, black game and hares – and not wildfowl, rabbits, pigeons and other species classed as vermin.

Another aspect of the law that should be understood by shotgun shooters is the Proof Acts, which require all firearms to be tested before being sold or exchanged. This testing is done in either the Birmingham or London Proof House, and the officially recognised marks are stamped on the barrels and action of weapons that pass the test. Britain has a reciprocal agreement with many other countries, whereby each country recognises all the others' proof testing methods and marks. However, there are notable exceptions to the countries involved – particularly the United States and Japan. It is an offence to attempt to sell a gun that is not 'in proof'. These few notes are only a brief guide to the laws that are most likely to affect you. However, the situation is really rather complicated, and there are severe penalties for breaking any firearms law. Furthermore, new laws are passed from time to time, and you should check with the police if you have any doubt at all.

NITRO PROOFMARKINGS

FEDERAL GERMAN REPUBLIC
(W. GERMANY)
Recognition was accorded in September 1955.

NITRO PROOF

N or

Other marks are used to indicate year of proof, bore diameter in millimetres, case length, etc., but such marks are always in addition to one or other of those shown above.

BRITISH
1954 Rules of Proof. (effective 1-2-55)

NITRO PROOF
London   Birmingham

MAGNUM
London   Birmingham

Additionally arms will bear markings to indicate the maximum mean pressure* of cartridges for which the arm has been proved together with the nominal gauge (in a diamond, as <>) and chamber length Shotguns will also bear marks to indicate the nominal bore diameter, as found at 9 in. from the breech, shown in decimals e.g. ·729 in.

*In exceptional cases maximum service loads may be marked in lieu of service pressures.

1925 Rules of Proof.

London   Birmingham

Rules of Proof prior to 1904.

Birmingham Company Proof words: NITRO PROOF

AUSTRIAN
Recognition was accorded in January 1956.
Proof Houses at Vienna and Ferlach.

NITRO PROOF

Voluntary additional reinforced proof (i.e. suitable for Magnum loads).

There are other marks used to indicate the quality of the barrel steel, the gauge of the gun, the bore diameter in millimetres, the case length, etc., but such marks are always in addition to one or more of those shown above.

FRENCH
Proof in France became compulsory only in July 1960.
Although there is a Proof House in Paris the majority of guns made in France will bear St. Etienne marks as listed below.

NITRO PROOF   SUPERIOR PROOF
(I.E. MAGNUM)

P.T.   P.T.

Other marks are used to indicate the gauge of the gun, the bore diameter and the length of chamber. The two latter will be shown in millimetres.

113

ITALIAN
Proof House at Gardone Val Trompia.

Additionally marks are impressed to show the proof year, the bore diameter in mm, the nominal gauge and the barrel weight in kilogrammes. There are other marks used but always in addition to the above mentioned.

BELGIAN
Proof House at Liege

Nitro Proof up to 1968	Superior Proof (i.e. Magnum) up to 1968

NITRO PROOF 1968 on	MAGNUM 1968 on

There are other marks used to indicate bore diameter and chamber length in millimetres, but they are always in addition to the above-mentioned.

In Belgium no alteration may be made of bore diameter without reproof. Furthermore, barrels are weighed and marked as to their weight at proof. Reduction in the weight of the barrels due for instance to enlargement or for any other reason may render the barrel out of proof.

Barrel weights are shown, for example: 1 kg 229.

CZECHOSLOVAKIAN
Accorded recognition in 1963.

Additional marks may indicate chamber length, degree of choke and year of manufacture.

SPANISH
Proof House at Eibar
Since July 1931 all arms

bear ... on barrel and action also ... and ... and

Other marks used indicate gauge, bore diameter and chamber length in millimetres, etc., but they are always in addition to those described above.

12 bore guns proved for Magnum loads are marked '1200 kg'.

IRISH
Recognised 1969.

Proof mark denotes both Provisional and Definitive Proof.

Additional markings indicate gauge and chamber length, nominal bore diameter, the service pressure for which the gun has been proved and the year of proof shown as the last two digits of that year.

Technical information

Percentage of total pellets in 30 inch circle

BORING OF GUN	RANGE IN YARDS								
	20	25	30	35	40	45	50	55	60
True cylinder	80	69	60	49	40	33	27	22	18
Improved cylinder	92	82	72	60	50	41	33	27	22
Quarter choke	100	87	77	65	55	46	38	30	25
Half choke	100	94	83	71	60	50	41	33	27
Three quarter choke	100	100	91	77	65	55	46	37	30
Full choke	100	100	100	84	70	59	49	40	32

Diameter of spread

BORING OF GUN	RANGE IN YARDS						
	10	15	20	25	30	35	40
True cylinder	20	26	32	38	44	51	58
Improved cylinder	15	20	26	32	38	44	51
Quarter choke	13	18	23	29	35	41	48
Half choke	12	16	21	26	32	38	45
Three quarter choke	10	14	18	23	29	35	42
Full choke	9	12	16	21	27	33	40

Forward allowance at various ranges

Bird crossing at 40 m.p.h., standard velocity cartridge

Range in yards	30	35	40	45	50
Forward allowance	5'6"	6'8"	8'0"	9'6"	11'1"

Useful addresses

The Birmingham Proof House
Banbury Street
Birmingham
B5 5RH

The British Association for
    Shooting and Conservation
National Headquarters
Marford Mill
Rossett
Clwyd
LL12 0HL

British Shooting Sports Council
Pentridge
Salisbury
Wiltshire
SP5 5QX

The Clay Pigeon Shooting
    Association
107 Epping New Road
Buckhurst Hill
Essex   IG9 5TQ

The Game Conservancy
Fordingbridge
Hampshire

The London Proof House
The Gunmakers Company
48 Commercial Road
London E1 1LP

Scottish Clay Pigeon Association
42 Hill Street
Tillicoultry
Central Scotland

Publications

The Field Carmelite House Carmelite Street London EC4Y 0JA	Weekly	*Shooting Times & Country Magazine* Burlington Publishing 10 Sheet Street Windsor Berkshire SL4 1BG	Weekly
The Shooting Handbook Beacon Publishing Jubilee House Billing Brook Road Weston Favell Northampton	Annual		
		Sporting Gun EMAP Publications Bretton Court Bretton Peterborough Cambridgeshire PE3 8DZ	Monthly
Shooting Magazine Burlington Publishing 10 Sheet Street Windsor Berkshire SL4 1BG	Monthly		

Index